# Return to Shandalee

### Confessions from Summer Camp: Woodstock, the Moon Landing, Racial Divide, Murder, Vietnam and Annie. A Story of Transformation and Redemption from 1969

## JF Krizan

This book is a work of historical fiction. The characters and events portrayed are either products of the author's imagination or are used fictitiously. Any resemblance to actual persons, living or dead, events, organizations, theories or locales is entirely coincidental.

# Dedication

Nearly everyone has heard the phrase, "The spirit is willing but the flesh is weak" (The Holy Bible, King James Version, New Testament, Matthew, Chapter 26, Verse 41). This book is dedicated to all of those who show us how to find reconciliation between spirit and flesh, between what we should do and what we want to do.

# Acknowledgements

All those that I knew made a significant contribution to the creation of this book. It is because of them collectively that it was possible. Some I knew for decades, others a few years, and still others, just weeks. My only regret is that I may not have fully understood the meaning or connection of many things through my early life. That is no longer the case.

I am also grateful for the cover art capturing the dream that was Shandalee. The creation of Sue Whitney Fine Art.

# Chapter Contents

 Chapter I

# On the Road to Roscoe

It was only my first week of work at Shandalee, in appearance a rather ordinary sleep-away summer camp nestled in the bucolic Catskill Mountains of New York. I was still trying to get to know the other kitchen boys; Bobby, Max and Drew. There was this guy Parrot too, just a few years older than us but in charge of our crew. He really ran the kitchen, but he mostly supervised the four of us. Chef, that's what he was mostly called, was this cranky, roly-poly, semi-retired man who made the menu and prepared all the meals along with his solitary younger assistant Warren. Then there was the baker, Karl, an odd guy who reported to James. In the kitchen, everyone reported to James, except Chef.

Since the camp was under two hour's drive from my home in Ridgewood, New Jersey it wasn't a big deal for me to ride up in my new car that I had bought for running around that summer of 1969, really not new. It was beat up far beyond its seven-year age; dents, dings, rust, faded blue paint, and barely worth the fifty bucks that I paid a neighbor, but it ran. I put four new tires on it, checked the oil, filled it up and off I went to spend an easy eight weeks before my enlistment in the Army became official.

It was winter of my high school senior year when I reached the conclusion to go for early enlistment, then sign when I turned eighteen in September following graduation. The whole process was rather simple; I took an aptitude test at the local recruitment office, then a physical preparedness test at Fort Dix, not too far off, still in New Jersey. Since I was graduating in June, my future was locked in, barring any unexpected circumstances. I just needed to find something to fill the summer, and a way to tell my parents of my decision to delay college.

Even though I had made some early noise about taking a break after high school they never took me seriously. It was earlier in the year, at dinner I remember, that I brought up the idea of taking an entry level job as a newspaper reporter to prepare me for a degree and career in writing or journalism. Dad, mostly him, had planned and hoped and dreamed that I would attend his alma mater, Cornell. The same place where he fell in love with a girl his freshman year, who he would later marry and become my mom. Being an only child didn't make it easier for any of us. Since I had no brothers or sisters through which he could relive his youth, his misdirected focus was solely on me. I always did my own thing, but also tried to do the *right* thing, for me that is; after all I had plans too.

It's not always easy to please everyone in your inner circle and stay true to yourself at the same time. Because of my reluctance to openly brush-off or disappoint my parents I had sent an admission application to Cornell in February and was accepted in March. Pretty quick I thought and yeah, I was somewhat surprised of their decision. It couldn't have been for my grades since I was now a solid "C" underachiever. Instead, I thought it mainly because of my college legacy parents, an admission system which rewards applicants whose parents or siblings attended. The fact that I had skipped fourth grade didn't seem to be a positive factor in Cornell's decision either. It certainly was no benefit or disadvantage to me when interacting with the other high school students. All it meant was that I was a year younger than most of

3

my classmates and graduating at seventeen, instead of eighteen. I didn't hardly shave either, never even able to grow the cool sideburns that I wanted. That aside, it seemed that colleges were more interested in SAT scores than character. My scores were noticeable; fifteen forty, that's sixty less than perfect, just saying. I let others be the judge of my "character."

There is no ideal time for bad news, so I waited a month to tell them about my early commitment to the Army. It went about as well as you would expect. Ruined our dinner that night, but after another month they began to get over it; what choice did I give them? More out of concern for my well-being than anything else, they asked about my plans for the summer. Good question! I thought about getting a job down at the Jersey shore, as a busboy or waiter, neither of which I had ever done, but how hard could that be? I imagined it to be a ton of fun, a bunch of young people from all over, descending on one of the most desirable beach vacation spots, briefly embracing communal living while taking full advantage of the notorious nightlife. I was already working at our public library, shelving returned books and retrieving patron-requested periodicals from the basement, also very easy and brainless. But, the library was not how I wanted to spend my last months before being sent off to Basic Training.

How this other summer job opportunity came about was rather haphazard; more luck and chance than careful planning. My friend, who worked with me at the library, told me about, "This cool summer job washing dishes," his words, not mine. I had known him for the three years in high school. Only three because high school really began at two other schools in town for our freshman year, what they call junior high, grades seven through nine. Since he went to the *other* junior high, we never met.

Still, he's all excited about this summer job he saw advertised in the local newspaper's Help Wanted section. Completely ignoring the fact that we would be washing dishes, he saw scheduling as the *only* problem. He went on to explain that he could only work the month of July, before he and his family packed up for their overseas summer vacation, nice, right? But, if I wanted to work August he thought that we could get it. Of course that meant that we would have to quit the library just prior to our intended job change schedule. I didn't say no and I didn't say yes, I needed much more information. So, seeing that I was skeptical, he ran downstairs with me following, and as I stood next to him, dialed his mother on the library payphone. Apparently she had been a long-time volunteer at the local United Christian Women's Association and knew all the administrators there. I heard of the place, like a YMCA, but everybody just called it the UCWA. My friend was thinking that her connections might be enough to land us jobs at the summer camp they sponsored. After telling her his scheme she promised to try to get us an interview appointment.

His mother came through and we had our meeting with UCWA Assistant Director Miss Ahearn that next morning, I had no idea how this was going to turn out, a long shot at best I thought. Regardless, I didn't like the idea of being stuck in a kitchen washing dishes. Miss Ahearn was so serious, stressed how important these jobs were, and how she would need to depend on all of the summer staff to do their part. Her description of the camp was not ordinary, her eyes seemed to glaze over at the very mention of the camp name, Shandalee. Like she was describing a recent dream, or something she loved, or the only thing she loved. I couldn't help but to feel sorry for this middle-aged woman whose gray hair and frail stature gave the appearance of someone much older and more worn from life itself. She went on until I was beginning to buy into the mystique of Shandalee. Then, I wanted to go, I just had to go!

When she agreed to hire us I was shocked; under our terms with the split schedule! The season was just two months away. What this really meant, as she explained, the both of us would be working in the kitchen at an *all-girls'* summer camp in Livingston Manor, New York, right in the center of all the Catskill's action. She thought nothing of informing us that the campers ranged in age from twelve to sixteen, the CIT's, high school girls seventeen to eighteen, and the counselors, all college girls eighteen to twenty-one. Did she not understand that we were boys, practically men, with lots of raging hormones! "Do you boys know what CIT's are? Feeling a need to reply I said, "No, can't say that I do Miss Ahearn." "It stands for Counselor-in-Training, now you know." Unbelievable that this was actually going to happen for us, it was hard for me to keep from bursting out in celebration.

Wow, I was going to spend my summer in the "Jewish Alps," a name well known from growing up in Northern New Jersey. I also heard it affectionately referred to as the "Borscht Belt." You see, those labels were derived from the decades that Jewish residents, living everywhere between New York City and Chicago, flocked to the hundreds of resorts, inns and camps in the Catskills. Many of those resorts, like Tamarack Lodge, Nevele Grand Resort Hotel, Brickman's, The Concord, Kutsher's and maybe the most famous of them all, Grossinger's Catskill Resort & Country Club, catered to these kosher clients. They were mainly families, but also included single young men and women seeking to meet other like-minded people. Me, I wasn't Jewish, but I couldn't hardly call myself a Catholic either since I only went to church on Easter and Christmas.

I passed the remaining time at school and library daydreaming about life after graduation, and was increasingly looking forward to going away to Shandalee. During the school-sponsored graduation festivities it was easy to run into my library friend who found us our summer job. For the record, I never really considered him a true friend, a bit too disingenuous for me and suppose I was still annoyed at him for the comment he made in signing my senior class yearbook;

*"Chris, I guess it's been fun knowing you"*

*"I guess?"* What the hell is that supposed to mean? If he wasn't a friend what was he? But forget that, it didn't end there, it got worse. He waits until graduation night to tell me that he's no longer available to work in July. I'm dumbfounded as he continued blathering on, "Before college I'm going to be spending the *entire* summer visiting my aunt and uncle in Switzerland. It's a once in a lifetime opportunity for me." Like I'm supposed to be happy for him, or impressed? Instead, I was in shock, trying my best to calculate in my head all of the probabilities of his announcement derailing my own summer plans.

I called him a *douchebag* probably ten times, I loved using that word and it fit him well. "You douchebag, did you call the camp lady yet?" "No, you should tell her, maybe you can go for the whole summer." What I did for the "whole summer" was not for him to decide. His change of plans was probably going to screw the entire thing up for me. After a few more choice words to him I abruptly disengaged myself from his stupidity. My last words, "You douchebag!"

It took me a couple of minutes to find my date Tink, who I had temporarily abandoned with all of our other fellow graduates in the large catering hall at Terrace on the Park. I hadn't been near this place since my parents took me to the 1964 New York World's Fair in Flushing, Queens. Being in New York, I thought it was an odd choice for a *New Jersey* high school graduation party. Nevertheless, I was feeling a bit nostalgic over the past memory. There was little else remaining at the former fair site, just the U.S. Steel Unisphere, I think.

I had to force myself to put aside my new problem, after all, this was graduation night! I spent the rest of the dinner and festivities laughing and talking to Tink about our future plans, which actually didn't include each other. That sounds so harsh, but she and I were just friends, nothing more. Despite my best effort, for the rest of the night I kept thinking about having to call the camp lady the second her office opened on Monday.

As it turned out, because of her business travel, I couldn't get her on the phone until Wednesday. I explained the turn of events and she was surprisingly calm, "I don't care one bit which of you is going to work and when, just as long as one of you works July *and* August."

Having made that perfectly clear, I asked if I could do both months. Miss Ahearn of course agreed, "Is there anything else? If not, I'll be sending you a letter with all the things that you need to know. See you at Shandalee, I'm the Camp Director up there so you'll see me a lot this summer. I hope there aren't going to be any more surprises before July." I was happy that my plans weren't totally screwed up, let my parents know, and never ran into the other library guy again, good riddance, douchebag!

From our second floor rooms in "The Big House," overlooking Lake Shandalee, all four of us kitchen boys had been coming down together at eight-thirty to set up for breakfast. Most of our work really began *after* the meals, with cleanup and dishes. Today however, Drew and I were the first staff to arrive, a little early. Since Drew says he's from Ohio, who knows how the hell he ever found this place. He seemed younger than the rest of us, physically, mentally, and maturity-wise I mean, and didn't know much about anything. Because of that he would regularly be left out of our conversations or our attempts to socialize with the younger counselors and CIT's.

Bobby, whose room was next to mine, always took longer before appearing in the morning, usually brushing his hair a hundred times while staring at himself in the bathroom mirror. Then, from the overpowering smell of his morning application of *English Leather* cologne you always knew he was near, way, way too much! He fancied himself a ladies man, I don't know why, maybe a little good looking, to the ladies I mean, and that's a *maybe*.

Max is a night owl, and haven't seen much of him outside the kitchen. I'm a light sleeper so I sometimes hear him coming in late, I mean like two or three in the morning, trying to tread lightly down the half-dark hallway leading to his bedroom. I don't even know how he manages to make it to breakfast, does he even sleep? He and Bobby were still attending Livingston Manor High School, with another year to go. They actually lived in town but during the summer they had to stay at The Big House, which was a requirement for our employment at Shandalee.

The Big House was no Holiday Inn! Yes, it was big, three stories, but having been built in the forties, the white wood clapboards were now cracked, warped and peeling, almost beyond repair. It actually looked like it had originally been a church, or meeting house or retreat of some kind because of the very tall and prominent white steeple projecting skyward in some outlandish symbolic statement connecting the earthbound with heaven. It was a very tall steeple. Any cross which might have topped it off was gone, but its bell remained, now clanging for every meal, calling all of us to gather, to eat and us kitchen boys to work.

What you saw on the outside was what you got on the inside, with one exception, the kitchen. Thankfully, it appeared to have undergone a recent renovation which resulted in a very clean, bright and efficient operation for all of us to work. But overall, the building was an old mess, the kind of thing that should have been bulldozed years ago.

Karl the weirdo baker always started his shift at five-thirty, enough time to bake all the day's bread, rolls, and pastries before the little campers arrived for breakfast. He was just a sleazy guy, jumpy in an agitated kind of way and never interacted with the rest of the kitchen staff, guess he thought he was too cool for any of us. It was better that he came in early so we didn't have to deal with him, he was that creepy to me, he made me nervous.

Parrot was always there before us too, but today it was unusual to see him pulling the last trays of rolls out of the oven. Still half asleep I asked, "Where's Karl today?" Thinking that I was funny, "Did you get a promotion?" "Karl doesn't work here anymore," he replied without looking up from his work. "I need to talk to you today, see me after breakfast," still looking down. "Am I in trouble?" "No, not at all, I have to do something and I need to know if I can depend on you." "Sure Parrot, whatever you say, I'm here to help." I wasn't kissing ass, I meant it, I liked Parrot.

After breakfast cleanup I found him in the back food pantry taking inventory, a little peculiar since I was told that the kitchen boys would be assisting him in that chore every Sunday after dinner. For now that was of little matter to me, either way, so I asked, "Can you talk now?" "Give me fifteen minutes, be cool, I'll meet you on the porch. I'm going to Roscoe, can you come?" "Sure, if I'm back for the lunch shift." "Meet me on the porch," he repeated. Obviously preoccupied, I left him alone, leaving through the kitchen, then dining room and center screen door onto the porch. I sat and waited on one of a dozen creaky old Adirondack chairs. I never knew if any one of them would collapse under my weight, but relied on the fact that I wouldn't have far to fall.

"Ready Chris?" It was Parrot now summoning me as he stepped onto the porch. "OK, I'm ready, do you want me to drive?" It would be my first time in Roscoe, so I really didn't know much about it or how to get there, but I thought it was straight out Route 17, the same road that got me from home to Shandalee. "You're funny Chris, we're walking, it will be good exercise for you, better get used to it, Basic Training will be ten times worse." It was kind of strange that he said that because I didn't want anybody at camp to know anything about my future plans. Then I remembered! Drew was the first kitchen boy that I met upon arriving, and while trying to befriend him I shared my enlistment plans. It now seems that Drew may be a bit of a gossip boy.

So off we went, walking. "Chris, in case nobody told you, here's the lay of the land. You already know that Livingston Manor is tiny, mainly First Citizens Bank, Manor Theater, Central Pharmacy, Jake's Hardware, Schweinfurth's Deli, Saint Aloysius Church, and the famous Tony's Tavern, that's it, not much else. If we need a larger variety of supplies for camp we go to Roscoe, ten minutes. Still more needed, we go to Liberty, you know Grossinger's, right? Only fifteen minutes. For big time supplies we go to Monticello, half an hour. John's in charge of all of that driving, he works for Miss Ahearn." Yeah, but he's talking about *drive* time, not *walk* time. Big difference between driving ten minutes and walking the three or four miles to Roscoe, one way! I appreciated hearing all this but I'm thinking let's pick up the pace or we won't even make it back for dinner. I still didn't know what he wanted of me. Since Parrot wasn't interested in driving or riding today, we just walked past my car in the staff parking lot and down the long driveway to the main road.

"Hey Parrot, why does this sign at the intersection with our driveway say "Hardscrabble Road PVT?" He laughed, "This will be my fourth summer working at Shandalee and I thought the same thing when I first saw it. What the heck is PVT? I'm thinking it's some kind of acronym, so I tried to figure it out, but nothing made sense. Then it occurred to me, 'PVT' means 'Private.' It's a very long walk down Hardscrabble Road, isn't it Chris? Then, in some places too much gravel, other places not nearly enough or bare, and always difficult to maneuver around all of those potholes. But still, I love this walk."

"I promise that we are going to have a very interesting summer at Shandalee, every summer is different, for me and everyone else. Many of us come back each year; repeat season campers become CIT's and then they become counselors. But some don't come back, I don't know what happens to them, it's like they lose their way, so it goes. But, everyone who knows Hardscrabble Road will be changed forever, it's something that you have to travel to get to Roscoe, or any other place. Sure, everyone has a different Hardscrabble Road, but this has been mine, now it will be yours too." I barely understood if he was still talking about our driveway or something more, but when Parrot was speaking everyone was likely to be listening.

I already thought that Parrot was a very neat kind of guy, but during our walk I discovered the depth of his knowledge and other things that are simply not learned in any school. There were also long periods of time when he didn't speak, who knows what he was thinking, still you could tell his mind was not idle. I'm sure he also had plans, but they were unknown to me, at least for now.

I had lot of friends from home who had nicknames, like Hawk, Eagle, Mole and Rat, mostly because they looked like those birds or animals. They didn't give themselves those names, they were given *to* them. But to call him Parrot? It didn't make any sense. He certainly didn't look like any parrot, actually he was a tall, handsome, athletic-built, light-skinned Negro. Everyone liked Parrot, a good story teller and kitchen boss too. He was simply very popular, among all the guys and girls at Shandalee.

I decided to break one of the periods of silence and asked, "How'd you get the name 'Parrot?'" He laughed, "I get that a lot, it's my name, my last name, Parrot, I'm James Parrot, my mother calls me Jimmy." I didn't feel so dumb because nobody ever called any of us by our last names, how could I have guessed? I was born Christopher Bronson, never had a nickname unless you consider Chris such a thing. I never thought that I looked like any barnyard animal or any other animal. "Chris, let me tell you something, you can call it a story, but to me it's my heritage, retold through the generations. When my first ancestor arrived in America he was sold to the owner of a rice plantation in Charleston, South Carolina. Not everyone grew cotton as a cash crop, sometimes tea or rice."

I knew history, but I didn't know about rice or tea, now too engaged in his story to ask any questions. "When slaves arrived their African names were almost always overlooked, ignored or simply replaced with something more European sounding," he explained. "At that time, the surrounding woods and trees down there were filled with Carolina parrots, something that delighted the plantation owner, I'm told. That's how my great-great-great grandfather got his name! James Parrot was his name." I'm speechless at this point hanging on his next word.

"The Carolina parrots are now extinct, hunted for their feathers for ladies hats, not one of them still living. Slavery was a sin, but *us* Parrots survived. Sorry to have bored you with all of this, I just wanted to explain something." "No, I'm glad that you told me, I don't know what to say." "You don't have to say anything, as a matter of fact, please keep it to yourself." "OK, OK," I said. "You know what Chris, I'd like it best if you call me James, that's what I like to be called, and maybe it will catch on back at Shandalee." "Sure, whatever you say, whatever you say, James."

As he noticed me checking my watch again, "Don't you be worrying about the time, I finished the baked goods for the day and the other guys will have to make up for your absence at lunch, we should be back in time for dinner." "What about Miss Ahearn? She'll know I'm gone when she does lunch?" "Don't worry about her, I've already told her that I needed you to go to Roscoe with me, don't worry as long as you're with me." So I'm thinking this is pretty cool, what a great day! James was now pacing us at a good clip, making our return by dinner likely.

"What did you want to talk to me about?" It appeared that he was giving his response some thought before speaking. "I'm not a ball-buster, it's not my nature, but I expect certain things from people, whether they work in the kitchen with me, or even people that I randomly meet, call them 'expectations.' It's particularly bothersome when a course of action they choose negatively affects *me*, and that's the problem with Karl." Hesitating, "*My* problem now. You know I order all the supplies for the kitchen and stuff just doesn't disappear, unless we eat it. It started last summer, I suspected Karl, confronted him and gave him a warning, now he's up to it again. This time no warning, I just told him of the consequences if he stayed, I'd get the police involved. I made myself quite clear. Yesterday he told Director Ahearn that he had a 'family emergency' which required him to return home for an extended period, just as I had advised him."

I appreciated his confiding in me but also understood that he was surely going to provide some explanation for our walk this morning. Finally, "I need you to replace Karl and do all the baking. I'll do it the rest of this week, you can watch how things are done, and then you can begin on Monday." It didn't seem like a very good deal for me but I let him continue. "After Karl would finish baking, part of his job was to hand wash all the pots and pans, they don't fit in the dishwasher. You do this for me, do the baking that is, and I'll have the other guys wash the pots and pans for you. Think about it, you may be starting at five-thirty but you're done at eight-thirty, and have the rest of the day to yourself. Chris, there's nothing much better than Shandalee during the summer, our lake is magnificent, two hundred forty acres I think. It's the early morning I like best, when you can hear the majestic screaming eagles striking down from the skies. Even the lowly raccoons have purpose as they wander around looking for scraps. I love it all!"

"Let me get this right, I'm now working two hours per meal per day, that's six hours a day, times six days a week since I get a day off, that's thirty-six hours a week and beginning next week you want me to work three hours a day times six days is eighteen?" "No, not quite, you won't have a backup so it will be seven days, means twenty-one hours." Parrot, I mean James, was not such an easy guy to refuse so I said, "OK, but don't let me screw up and burn the peperoni rolls, they're a camp favorite." He laughed, "Thanks Chris."

Soon we arrived in Roscoe, really not much bigger than Livingston Manor. When we came upon this convenience store James asked me to wait for him out front, then went in alone. I watched as he walked to the back of the small store selling groceries and other sundry items. It was impossible to hear what he was saying to this one store guy but you could tell the guy wasn't liking it. James appeared calm and cool as usual while the guy was flailing his arms and strutting around in small circles, looking like a crazed rooster. His kooky gyrations stopped abruptly, now still, just listening to James. Five minutes and he was out. "What was that all about?" "Nothing, but that's what happens when you go into business with half-witted people like Karl. He also quieted down when I mentioned the police."

"Come on, I'll buy you lunch!" Lunch? It turned out that James had a sweet tooth, and bought us the biggest and best banana splits from counter service at Kresge's down the block. After spending a half hour there, we each bought a big bag of pistachio nuts and left. We were always eating those little red-shelled nuts around The Big House, who knows how many pounds each of us would eat that summer. Eating pistachio nuts was just another kitchen boy tradition started years ago, another thing which set us apart from everyone else at camp. They were good, but almost too good, rather addicting I found. Who would have guessed that I would find a great deal of personal satisfaction that summer belonging to this offbeat crew, "The Kitchen Boys?"

I was glad to be able to walk my sundae off on our return to Shandalee. James continued to tell me stories of his family and home town, Paterson, New Jersey, not too far from my home but a million miles different than my life growing up. Almost back now and wanting to change the subject he asked, "What's up with you and Annie, you like her, don't you?" "Yes, she's a really nice girl."

 Chapter II

# The Front Porch

"Annie?" I don't even understand why he would say such a thing! I had just met her the day before, but at that time I didn't know anything about James little ally Ruby and unaware of the super-speed, well established, Shandalee gossip network. Good luck in trying to keep *anything* private. Every day before lunch, a half hour before, us Kitchen Boys would gather on the porch to socialize, mainly with the female camp staff of course. Janie, one of the more outgoing CIT's, a real talk-a-too, would bring her campers up early so she could also flirt around. There were also other counselors who came early, like Beth, who so reminded me of the TV phenom Tiny Tim with his falsetto voice and long brown curly hair, I mean very long. The sun always seemed to shine at Shandalee and sitting on the porch talking or just watching the bee hive of camper activity swarming up the lawn in search of a meal was a wonderful way to pass my time.

The porch covered the whole front of The Big House and through three green floppy screen doors you could get anywhere inside. That made the porch the best place to hang out before our kitchen shifts. Through the screen door on the right, you could usually see Miss Ahearn's super-cute, untouchable, twenty-something secretary, Gina, guarding the Camp Director's office; Miss Ahearn's private sanctuary where she conducted all of the camp business, or retreated for some much needed quiet time. Although the UCWA provided the Director with an apartment in Livingston Manor I think that she spent most nights sleeping on a cot that was said to be within her office.

There was an additional office, the nurse's office, treating anything from bee stings to sunburn. It was in Gina's outer office that campers frequently lined up to use the two pay phones, mostly calls to home. Yes, some were homesick, but most were just so excited to tell their parents how much fun they were having at Shandalee. I never could understand why some of the campers, not many, maybe three or four, felt so alienated, alone, or scared that they had to be picked up by mid-session. If the other campers were to ever ask Miss Ahearn why they left she provided them with her standard response, "They had contracted pink eye, something that is very contagious." Clearly, Miss Ahearn did not want an epidemic of "home sickness," which could be a problem with no easy treatment. True, each camper was signed up for one of two sessions, a month long, July or August, which could simply be too much for some of them to handle, especially if they had never been away. To me, it was shaping up as the place to be in the summer of 1969; how could it possibly be better anyplace else?

Through the screen door on the opposite end was "The Lodge" where The Kitchen Boys, counselors and CIT's met almost nightly. There was nothing like it, the most comfortable, interactive social gathering space that I had ever come across anywhere. Like an altar is the centerpiece to a church, a massive fieldstone fireplace was the heart of The Lodge. The round stones the size of melons covered the wall, carefully laid to reach the top of the cathedral ceiling, probably eighteen feet, if not more. There were well used couches and upholstered chairs spread throughout, tables for cards and the numerous board games available, and thread-bare oriental carpets to hide the well-worn floors. Barely illuminating our evenings was a gargantuan hanging chandelier made of antlers and pine cones, not a few, but hundreds. Many of the dozen bulbs had burned out which accounted for the dim lighting in the room. Old dusty pictures of fish, fishing, wild game, and hunting covered the walls in between the stuffed and mounted heads watching over us.

Not all of the counselors or CIT's would be there every night because somebody had to be supervising the campers after "lights out" at nine-thirty. From The Lodge the entire kitchen staff, Handyman the camp fixit guy, and driver John climbed the stairs to their bedrooms on the second floor. Us Kitchen Boys never really spent too much time in our rooms except to sleep. They were bare bones; bed, nightstand, tiny closet, and a single dresser. Absolutely nothing like my room at home.

It was just Wednesday or Thursday of the first week of camp when Beth brought up her bongo drums to have some pre-lunch fun on the porch. She played them for a bit, laughed with us, then passed them to Max who was surprisingly very, very good. James walked out, "What's going on?" "Just having some fun Parrot, they're mine, wanna try?" "Sure!" He banged out five minutes of something like it was right off a record and when done, just smiled and said, "How was that?" We actually hooted and howled and clapped, James was that entertaining. What a showman, maybe the only thing that Max seemed to lack compared to James, showmanship. "You're next Bobby," as he handed the bongos off and returned inside, his curiosity satisfied. Bobby held his own, and then what I dreaded from the beginning, he passed them to me. I earnestly tried, but regrettably I have no rhythm whatsoever, but my friendly audience nodded their approval anyway.

The bongo concert now ended, a couple of campers came over to socialize, really not such an unusual occurrence. From day one I had been amazed how everyone, campers, CIT's, counselors, The Kitchen Boys, James, Warren, and John all hung out together, no discernable cliques, much different than the tedious social structure of Ridgewood High School. Now standing among us, this one camper turned her eyes to me and asked, "Where you from?" Bobby jumped right in there, "Max and me are from Livingston Manor, I'm Bobby." Not wanting to hear the rest of his unwanted boy-pitch, she interrupted, "Let him answer," pointing to me. We all chuckled at her spunk, and Bobby's put-down, something which he probably wasn't used to.

To be honest, from the first day of camp I had noticed her among all the others. She was vaguely familiar but yet I had no recollection of ever meeting her before then. She was very attractive, but more like a college girl, not a teenager, looking the part of the "girl next door" that everyone wants to be with. But, since she was a camper she had to be between twelve and sixteen. I'm thinking sixteen. She had the looks more like a counselor, not even the CIT's were built like her, they all looked younger. Her brown skin and sun-streaked hair was more fitting the end of the summer at the Jersey shore, not early July in the Catskills.

I was momentarily paralyzed and baffled by the undeserved attention directed at *me*. Her last words echoing in my head, "Let him answer." Sounds so simple, but sometimes it's not easy when you tend to be cautious, or maybe just on the shy side. "Ridgewood, New Jersey, ever hear of it?" From her singular ordinary question, I immediately felt a strong connection with this person, this girl, this seemingly special girl. "Wow, me too." "Hi, I'm Chris Bronson." I knew your name, one of the other girls had told me. I'm Annie Ward, nice to finally meet you." "Me too."

From that moment, the group conversation was going to be monopolized by the two of us; what streets we lived on, had we ever been here before. I even knew exactly where she lived, I had passed it many times. A picture perfect street with stately homes and lush lawns, unofficially called "Doctors Row," very close to the hospital, and high school farther down. It turned out that we had no common friends, nor had I ever seen her before at school. "How come I never saw you in high school?" "Because I haven't gotten there yet, I'll be a sophomore starting in September." "And I just graduated!" We laughed but I'm thinking, how old is she? "I know what you're thinking, well I'm fifteen, turning sixteen the second week of school." "When?" "The twelfth." "Very cool, I'm the tenth, turning eighteen." Now she's looking directly at me as she mouths the words, "Close enough." Wow, what does she mean by that? Should I be worried?

The others in our small group quickly lost their interest in our mundane jibber-jabber, boring to them, and got up to find something more appealing to do, and I had to go in to start kitchen dishes soon. But I liked Annie and could have talked to her all day. Suddenly, as she looked at her watch, "Oh my gosh! I've got to go, I'll be late for swimming lessons, I'll eat later, see you at dinner Chris," jumping up from her chair and leaping down the rickety wooden steps. I watched as her little white Keds flew down the long narrow paved path to the sandy beach at the lake. Something was happening here, and it was good. I hadn't even heard the lunch bell, but due to the fact that Annie and I had been the only ones remaining on the porch it was now obvious that I had to also get inside to prepare for cleanup. From that day until the end of the first session, I spent much of my time thinking about her and planning how we could spend a few minutes together in between all of our scheduled work and activities. I soon discovered that she was doing the same.

I had already told the other Kitchen Boys about James' request of me to replace Karl, changing my hours and relieving me from washing dishes and routine kitchen cleanup. Even though Drew complained that they would be shorthanded without me, Bobby and Max were more bummed out that our band of brothers was going to be broken up. After considering all things, and not wanting to miss out on any of our Kitchen Boy fun I talked it over with James and he approved my request to do both jobs, as baker and Kitchen Boy. I simply did not care about the early morning rise or extra hours, good preparation for Basic Training in two months I thought! There was to be no extra money for me, but that was fine.

Anticipating another visit with Annie before dinner, I was struggling how I was going to tell her that I would be enlisting immediately after camp ended, making any relationship together rather impossible. I understand that someone may think that I'm just another goofy guy getting way ahead of himself after meeting a girl for the first time. It is not my nature to be impulsive or irrational, I ponder things far too long. Even in high school lunch I found it necessary to consider all the pros and cons for buying either an open faced meatloaf sandwich with gravy and potatoes or chicken a la King on any given day. My telling Drew about enlisting was stupid on my part, but this is something that I thought Annie needed to know, it was only fair to her, and to me.

By my senior year I had grown very weary of school and the tidy little box that the class structure and prescribed curriculum carefully placed me in. When I was asked to write my senior history term paper we were restricted to one of ten topics; that was it. Having to choose one, I chose "War is Hell," why the heck not? I would have preferred to write about something else, of my own creation! That might be a meager explanation of why I turned my paper in two months late. A box I say! I wanted to do *my* thing, make money, accomplish something; anything. I fulfilled my obligations at school, barely graduating, and at times, they would even grade me, "Poor But Passing."

Even the required reading that was so carefully chosen for all of us students never gave me a sense of any practical reality. My previous jobs stocking shelves at Macy's and Food King, and then the library were a greater reality to me. Seemed like everyone just *had* to read "*Of Mice and Men*," "*Catcher in the Rye*," "*Lord of the Flies*," "*To Kill a Mockingbird*," and "*You Can't Go Home Again*" by Thomas Wolfe. I'm lost to tell you how any of them changed my life or gave me a perspective which I had never before considered. They were just books, *their* books, and I believed that they would never be *my* story, *my* legacy or *my* philosophy. I wanted to *do*, not just *be*, the latter being easier, and also requiring very little effort. I needed to engage with the world around me, I was ready! How do you tell someone all that in fifteen to thirty minutes, time that I might have with Annie before the dinner bell clangs? It wasn't going to be easy.

It soon became routine for me to meet Annie on the porch before every breakfast, lunch and dinner. Before breakfast was probably my most favorite time together. I'd rise early and take my shower, mostly just to wake myself up, but also to make myself look more human for her. Somehow, during sleep, my normally fine, straight, Beatle-style haircut would be transformed into something resembling spikes of overgrown grass, dead grass, sticking straight up. No amount of greasy *Dixie Peach Hair Pomade* or even my mother's hair spray could ever tame it; I'd tried. Soap and shower was the only morning cure. It wasn't so easy to shower at The Big House. The camp's three cleaning ladies had exclusive use of the rooms and showers on the third floor, and the rest of us on the second floor had to use the outdoor showers. We had our own bathroom on the floor, just no showers.

Outside there were four hot showers, with wooden stalls built around them, leaving your head and shoulders and below your knees visible to anyone interested. Since they were located in the back of the building, there really weren't any spectators. By the time I got upstairs again to finish dressing and got down to the porch my hair would have air-dried. I forgot to pack a comb with me, so I never really looked my best, but I guess I looked just fine to Annie. Anytime during breakfast duty I would always try to peek out the kitchen door to catch a glimpse of her. After the daily camp announcements everyone was entertained by the singing of the camp anthem, a rousing version of some kind of primitive chant, so I was told. It would commence with all of the campers banging their hands in rhythm on their tables. Then Beth or one of the other counselors would start singing the first few lines. The others would quickly join in, first softly, then louder, then hootin' and howlin' their lungs out. After a week, half of the campers would be leaping from their seats to dance to the song, including my Annie. It was just so neat to watch!

**"Kumala kumala kumala vista**
**Kumala kumala kumala vista**

**Oh no no no na vista**
**Oh no no no na vista**

**Eenie meanie de-se meanie**
**Oh ah la eenie meanie**

**Eenie meanie de-se meanie**
**Oh ah la eenie meanie**

**Eenie meanie de-se meanie**
**Oh ah la eenie meanie**

**Beat to the oh ko ko na vista**
**Rah rah shhh...bah bah shhh"**

Bobby was a real storyteller, he loved an audience. Weekend nights in The Lodge were always a lot of fun, much more than I ever had in Ridgewood. Sure that Bobby felt the same way, here at Shandalee he was a big shot, at least that's how I think he saw himself. Home life for Bobby was another matter. Max eventually let us new guys know that if we ever got in trouble around Livingston Manor Bobby's father could help us out. As police chief, he typically made parking or speeding tickets disappear for his friends and family. Bobby's love for summer living at Shandalee also had a lot to do with his father. Max described him as a jovial, baby-kissing, hand-shaking public servant when visible around town, but at home, he was a bitter, divorced, failed single father who seemed to enjoy knocking Bobby or aiming criticism at him. "I never heard him give any praise for his accomplishments, like for baseball and football, sports in which he lettered at Manor High. He loves it here because he hates living at home." I remember Max's words very well, so harsh.

One Friday night there were bunches of us sitting around The Lodge, a lot of the counselors and Janie, the CIT who is now always flirting with Bobby. Believe me, he loved the attention. Bobby started talking about last year at Shandalee and this guy Stevie Ray Jones. "For those of you who weren't here last year you might not have heard about the exploits of Stevie Ray. He's in high school with Max and me and all three of us were working here. The raccoon problem at the garbage pen was much greater than now so he and a local friend of his came up with a scheme to reduce the raccoon population," causing the girls in the room to cringe and moan. "His plan was so secret that Max and me didn't even know about it." The pen was just the fenced in area about a hundred feet from The Big House, holding the garbage for pickup by the local trash collector. Without the fence, the scavenging raccoons would have eaten everything except the empty tin cans. The problem would have been completely eliminated if the pen had been built with a chain link top, as were the sides.

Bobby now has everyone's attention. "Way late one night Stevie Ray and his buddy took one of the old garbage cans and made a raccoon trap at the pen. Over a few kitchen scraps, they placed the can, and used a notched stick to prop it up a few inches, just enough to give the unsuspecting scavengers room to get at their meal." "Hurry up with your story Bobby," someone yelled out. "I'm getting there, just wait a minute. The trap was now set! They took a long ball of string and tied one end to the stick, the rest they unraveled to their hiding spot a few yards away, where they waited." I could tell that Bobby had told this story a dozen times, it sounded so rehearsed.

"It didn't take long for the first dinner guest to show up, a big fat raccoon, with eyes which seemed to glow in the dark." "Really Bobby? We got it," Max was now getting impatient. "Now peaceably feeding on the garbage under the can, Stevie Ray yanked the string, which dislodged the stick, which caused the can to trap the raccoon underneath. Now unable to escape, it allowed the guys to take the lid and carefully slide it under the can so that they could then turn it right side up. But, it didn't end there. After removing the lid to see their victim, get ready for this, they threw a coffee can filled with kerosene on the raccoon and lit it!" At this point I think some of the girls were going to puke and I felt about the same. "I wasn't there but Stevie Ray said it was screaming like a baby. Two sickos right? Unexpectedly, the raccoon tipped the can over, and although still on fire, started chasing him around the pen."

"Somehow in all the chaos his pant leg caught on fire, and now he was the one wailing. The raccoon ran into the woods and the other guy was able to put out the pants fire with his jacket. First thing the next morning, he goes to the nurse here to have his second degree burn treated, some really bad blisters, but very treatable. So, he tells the nurse what happened, she tells Miss Ahearn, and she tells Stevie Ray he's fired. Crazy story, right? All true!" Impressed with his tall tales, Janie spent the rest of the night yapping with Bobby. I'm glad Annie wasn't here to listen to this nonsense!

# Chapter III
# **Southern Comfort**

Even though the drinking age was eighteen in New York, and none of us Kitchen Boys were legal, Bobby and Max had been telling us about Tony's Tavern for weeks. It wasn't about the booze. Bobby said that he could get us whiskey or beer anytime we wanted, from his older brother he bragged. The two guys couldn't stop talking about Tony's famous roast beef sandwiches, right here in Livingston Manor. It was one of those nights when it was quiet in The Lodge, only a few of the CIT's where there. Noticeably absent were The Lodge regulars; Beth, Ellen, Sally, Sherry, and Kirsten. Something else must be going on somewhere. Anytime after dinner and before lights out the CIT's and counselors would hold camp-wide sing-alongs down at The Playhouse by the lake, maybe that's where they were. The Playhouse wasn't like the Manor Theater in town, but more like a barn with a makeshift stage and rows and rows of wood benches, enough to hold a hundred campers. On any given night you could hear them singing all the way up to The Big House.

Seeing no action in The Lodge, Bobby grumbled, "This blows, let's walk down to Tony's for something to eat, it's only 8:00, we've got plenty of time and I'm getting hungry again." Seeing Drew just sitting there looking bewildered I just had to ask, "Drew, don't you want to come with us?" I'm thinking, he's just fifteen, a really young fifteen if you know what I mean, and this may not be his thing. Hearing no response, "Warren, how 'bout you, want to take a walk to town?" "No thanks, I'm going to take it easy tonight, probably read." But that was Warren, although he lived with us in The Big House he liked to keep to himself mostly, except when it came to Kirsten. She was a senior

33

counselor, a rather quiet college co-ed who befriended Warren from the beginning. Many times I would see them in the evening, sitting on the front porch talking, just talking. Still, it was unusual for me to see a Negro and a white girl so compatible. While they were *outside* the rest of us sought our fun and entertainment *inside* The Lodge, making a ton of noise while blasting the record player.

I was glad to be doing something with The Kitchen Boys tonight, especially tonight. A week ago, a bunch of us staffers were in The Lodge chatting it up. At one point I was talking to Sally and the subject of going to the movies came up. For weeks everyone had been listening to the song *Mrs. Robinson*, a cut from one of our most often played albums, *Bookends*, by *Simon & Garfunkel*. Since I knew that *Mrs. Robinson* was the title song in the movie still out, '*The Graduate*,' and maybe because I thought it was a contemporary subject well suited for me, maybe about me, I simply said, "I'd like to see it when I get back to Ridgewood." Unexpectedly she replied, "Let's go see it next Sunday, it's at the Manor Theater, that's a good day for me." "Sure, that sounds cool," what was I supposed to say? So, tonight was supposed to be *our* movie night!

After those words left my lips I start thinking, did she just ask me out on a date and did I just say yes? True, she was one of the nicest counselors, already going to college, and even though she and all the rest of the counselors were clearly more mature and intelligent than The Kitchen Boys, they thought nothing of mixing it up with us. They were being friendly, that's all. I suppose I was intimidated by her and would have said yes to anything she asked. But, if I was going to be spending time alone with any girl at Shandalee it was going to be with Annie. I saw Sally around the camp several times during the week but I didn't bring the movies up again, hoping that she forgot about it.

As Bobby, Max and I were halfway through the door, Drew jumped up, "Wait for me!" I was glad that he was coming with us, probably because I sometimes felt guilty that we ignored him in The Lodge and hardly ever invited him to do anything with us, for good reason. A little bit later, I would again wonder about his loyalty. It was really just a short distance to Tony's and was a beautiful moonlit night to be out for a walk. Judging from all the cars they were packed, and they were. Still, I thought it surprising to be so busy on a Sunday night. We were lucky to find a table near the bar, surrounded by all of Tony's happy patrons, all sorts of people, younger, older, rough looking, well dressed; pretty cool!

Believe it or not, this was actually the first time that I'd ever been in a bar, I had no idea what really went on in one. It's not that I'm opposed to drinking but my time hadn't come yet. The legal age in New Jersey was twenty-one, so unless I was willing to get a fake ID, I couldn't be served. I spotted a couple of the counselors but don't think they even saw us come in. Funny, the place is packed but no juke box blasting, a rather quiet crowd I thought. Mostly everyone was focused on the three TV's mounted to the walls, not what I had expected in a bar like this. Then the light bulb goes off in my head, this is July 20th, this is the moon landing! Of course practically the whole world knew about the scheduled moon walk. It's just that when you're at Shandalee, not much going on anywhere else in the world seems to matter, it's extraordinary, not just for me, for all of us, almost *magical* in a word.

Maybe it's Annie, or James, but maybe it's the whole thing. Lately I haven't been thinking about Vietnam, the war or even my enlistment. I'm finding some inner peace here thinking about Annie nearly all the time.

I leaned over to the next table and asked what time they thought the moon walk was going to start. "Around midnight," they replied, "Hours from now." "Thanks, I think we'll be gone by then." As the nice, young waitress came over, "Yes, what can I get you?" "Hi Julie!" Bobby seemed to know her, but probably was just showing off to us guys. Ordering for all of us, "Four roast beef sandwiches please." "What to drink?" At the same time, all at once we said, "Coke." There is no way that any of us wanted to get into any underage drinking hassle thing, the two guys recognizable from town, Drew only fifteen and me being two months from legal in New York, still none legal. The sandwiches were quick to arrive with a mountain of French fries on each platter and a pickle spear. The guys were right, this was the best roast beef sandwich that I ever had; the freshest poppy seed roll with two inches of shaved medium-rare roast beef. Tasted like there was also salt and pepper and some kind of horseradish mayonnaise sauce. I smothered my fries with ketchup and went at it.

Even among us, Max was not a talker, but as the rest of us were very busy devouring our sandwiches it was clear that he really wanted to ask us something. He kept starting, but seemed to retreat upon seeing that no one was paying any attention to him. So I stopped chewing long enough to ask, "What's up with you Max, do you want to say something?" "Yeah, thanks Chris, I've been trying to tell you all for a few days now, since I found out myself. I'll tell you on the way back, it's nothing." Feeling uneasy about the way he said it, I asked, "Is there something wrong with you." Laughs, "No not like that, it's actually good news." I don't know how much Bobby knew of this but he didn't even look up as he finished the last of his fries. Now interested, "What did you say Max?" "I'll tell you later." "Then let's head out, I've got a present for us." It's like he wasn't even listening, especially about the news from Max. Done, we all agreed to leave. Just making small talk I simply said, "Maybe we'll make it back to The Lodge to watch the moon walk." But Drew, always the know-it-all, informed us, "I tried to turn the TV on the other night and pure static. I don't think it's even connected to the antenna, I couldn't get anything." In view of Max wanting to make some kind of announcement, the moon walk was not a high priority right now, at least not for me.

We paid up and were barely out the door as Max continued, "Bobby knows that I'm the manager of a local garage band called *Sackcloth*. They're mainly my high school friends. I was one of the founding members and used to play but after we got some good publicity last summer we needed help on the business side of things. That's what I've been doing since then. Because we've been getting a lot of jobs I'm not always around at night and come in late, I'm working. Plus, because we don't really make enough money to add more people I've been doing the sound and stage setup too. That's fine because I'd rather be doing those kinds of things than performing."

I could easily understand all of this, it made a lot of sense, coming in late and all. We already knew that he had a lot of musical talent; on the bongos and his dead on impersonation of *Doors'* front man Jim Morrison. Like his idol, he could sing the long ballads or turn *Light My Fire* into his own spirited version, pretty far out. Max was always singing in the kitchen, I'm not sure if he knew how good he was. Max continued to explain, "I got a call last week and now it's final, *Sackcloth* will be the opening act for *Vanilla Fudge* at Grossinger's! I'm a big fan of theirs, you know the song, *You Keep Me Hanging On*. I need, I mean I would really appreciate you all coming with me that night." "Wow, Max this is fantastic, what's there to think about? I'm in!" We all agreed!

Killing Max's moment Bobby says, "Wanna have some fun?" "I've got some *stuff* hidden in the woods. Let's take my shortcut to Hardscrabble Road. It's going to be a gas!" Max was quick to reply, "There isn't any shortcut, don't get us lost." Nobody was in the mood to argue with Bobby tonight, so we just humored him, like we did half the time. Sure everyone was thinking the idea of hiking through the woods to save a little time was unnecessary and dumb, and maybe dangerous since the sun had set a while ago and who knows what kind of animals we could meet along the way, probably scavenging raccoons or bears, who knows? After a little while of stumbling along his little-travelled path he stops, reaches up to the crotch of a tree limb and takes something down. "Did any of you ever hear of *Southern Comfort* whiskey?"

I'd heard of it, my grandfather's preferred beverage mixed with ginger ale, so just said, "Yup." I said it more in a way like dismissing it as ordinary, not like you're so cool, he wasn't. Bobby opened the half empty bottle, a rather large bottle, signifying that he'd probably made the trip from Shandalee several times, it also explained a lot. After taking a gulp, he lets out this loud grunt, like he swallowed something bad, yet exclaimed, "That's good stuff." I wish that he hadn't passed the bottle to Drew, it's just that he's so weak and would do anything to prove himself as a Kitchen Boy. Sure enough, Drew takes a similar sized gulp and also lets out a big hoot, imitating Bobby. Max was next then me. This really wasn't my thing, but wanted to go along to get along; not a philosophy I normally followed. I have to admit, I liked the taste of his booze, really sweet, but smelled like a bottle of perfume, but I don't really know what I'm talking about.

We continued to stand in a small circle, Bobby mostly bragging about his exploits with booze, and then girls, to the point where I knew that half of what they were claiming was made up. I don't even think that Drew had ever been on a date, and would bet that he'd never been kissed by a girl. Still, we all laughed after each story. Soon the bottle was empty and we just left it there on the ground. Once again, we proceeded along the path following Bobby. It was just a couple hundred yards more until we reached Hardscrabble Road. When finally out of the woods we all let out a big cheer.

It was pretty evident now that we were all a little tipsy, not so able to walk in a straight line, especially Drew. Our mood quickly changed as we saw headlights coming from the direction of The Big House. Barely audible, Bobby whispers what we're all thinking, "If it's Ahearn we're screwed, what a bummer." Almost upon us and too late to scatter and run since the moonlight, and now the headlights, had fully exposed us all, we're dead meat. "Shit, it's Miss Ahearn," Bobby concluded. "Wait a minute," as he takes a closer look, "That's her car, but it's Gina!" "It's Gina, it's Gina," we all start yelling to her like a bunch of school boys as she stopped in front of us. "What are you Kitchen Boys doing out so late, shouldn't you all be in bed?" It's just the way that she said it that was so sexy, Gina was a real fox, and when she spoke everyone just shut up. It was an honor that she was even acknowledging the existence of us juvenile delinquents, let alone talking to us. We all just about died when she got out of the car.

"You scared us, why are you driving Miss Ahearn's car, where's yours? I'm confused." "Chris, you're funny, I was in Miss Ahearn's office with a couple of the counselors watching the moon walk, it's over now. So I go to leave and my tire is flat. Since John wasn't available to fix it tonight Miss Ahearn said I could take her car." Obviously feeling the effects of the *Southern Comfort*, Bobby tells her, "Keep talking, don't stop, I love to hear you talk." Gina had to know that we'd all been drinking, especially after Drew had launched himself across the hood of the car to get a closer look at her.

"Can I have a goodnight kiss?" "Of course you can Drew," and delivered one on his cheek. I'm in shock as she leaned over and gave one to Max and then Bobby, just a peck like she gave Drew. Before I knew what was happening she reached up behind my head and pulled me to her to plant a major league, full-tonged one on my lips, a full out kiss, a long, time-stopping, girlfriend kind of kiss. I tried to keep my lips closed as she tried to come in. "What's the matter Chris, never been kissed by a girl before? She was still smiling at me as the other guys were yucking it up over the whole thing. I was speechless, feeling a bit embarrassed that I let it happen. But really, some girl just grabs you and lays one on, how is that my fault? Of course I was thinking about Annie. As Drew slid off the front of the hood Gina got back into the car, "Try to behave yourselves men."

We stood in a line, practically at attention, as she continued down Hardscrabble Road. "Chris, did you hear that, she called us 'men.'" "Just for tonight Drew, just for tonight, tomorrow we'll see." Then Drew blurts out, "If Aunt Sue could only see me now." It's the kind of comment that most people would not even pay attention to, just kind of like somebody reminiscing or talking out loud. But not me, "What did you say?" "Never mind, it's nothing." "No, I think it's something, what are you saying, better tell us." "It's supposed to be a secret, but 'Miss Ahearn' is my aunt, Aunt Sue. She's the one who got me this job." Bobby, quickly realizing all the risks, warned him, "You better keep your mouth shut about this or I'm going to beat you so hard that even your hair will hurt." Instead of cowering to Bobby, he yells back, "What kind of dirtball do you think I am! If she found out she'd be calling my mother in ten seconds and then I'd really get it." Us three other guys just laughed and from this special moment we all knew Drew was one of us too, after all was said and done, he was a Kitchen Boy!

# Chapter IV
# **The Game**

We knew that James was a pretty good basketball player, he had already beaten all of us one-on-one and always won at cut throat, just another kind of free-for-all game. There weren't enough staff guys to have a real full court game with five-on-five, John didn't play and it simply wasn't Warren's thing. When I was thinking and saying how neat it would be to have more players I considered asking the camp counselors to join in. Since us guys couldn't reach a decision about making it co-ed we never mentioned it to them. James had a better idea. Because he was a volunteer coach at the Livingston Manor Catholic Youth Organization, CYO he called it, he suggested that we invite his team to play us. We all thought it was a fantastic idea, so he did!

James and the rest of us Kitchen Boys were looking forward to the "big game." We actually practiced! Since there were only the five on our team we knew that each of us had to play the whole game, which could be tough. First team to score forty points wins. The CYO team turned out to be very competitive but with James playing on our team we had the slight advantage. Unfortunately, while The Kitchen Boys were leading thirty-five to thirty, I sprained my ankle on an easy layup. It was bad and felt like I was going to pass out as James led me off the court and sat me down. "Here, have some water, it's my thermos bottle, will you drink from my cup?" "Thanks James." Even though I wouldn't be returning to the game the others were able to finish, but hard to win four-on-five. CYO won forty to thirty-seven. Except for James, they were clearly better than the rest of us. Afterwards, Bobby told us a couple of them were playing for the Livingston Manor varsity team, figures.

The game had ended just as the sun was beginning to set over Shandalee and as much as I wanted to get back to The Big House and get off my foot, I had a different plan in mind. This was the night of the weekly campfire and I was dying to go, to see Annie of course. Maybe needing some help, I asked the other guys to come with me, "We'll only have to get out there later to put out the fire and clean up." Jimmy excused himself and walked off in the other direction to The Big House. Bobby laughed, "I know what you're up to, you want to see Annie, don't you?" Drew jumped right in there to try to mock me but I just ignored him, but he was absolutely right, I wanted to see Annie.

Max grabbed me by the arm and told the others, "Let's go, it's either now or later anyway." They helped me walk the hundred yards into the woods where we had set up the campfire earlier in the day with plenty of firewood, benches and water to douse the fire. All the way from the basketball court we heard them carrying on, already singing and laughing mostly. Our arrival was not noticed so much as we took seats in the back. Actually, where I was directing us to sit, a few feet behind the older campers, a few feet behind Annie, now almost in front of me. Within a few minutes she noticed us and scooted back a few feet, then I carefully shifted forward, trying not to draw attention to my sore ankle. We were now kind of sitting next to each other.

"Hi Chris, I was hoping you were coming." I felt the same way. I knew that Annie was special, uniquely connected to me, the degree to which I would discover later. It was unfortunate that being together at Shandalee was mostly limited to the porch and special events like this; how could we possibly develop a relationship this way? At times I had to really consider my intentions. She wasn't even sixteen, she was fifteen, three more years of high school, and I was probably going to Vietnam soon; how's that going to work? The realities of our future circumstance couldn't be more against us. Even the newly elected President, Richard Nixon, found that withdrawal wasn't going to be as easy as he believed when he was campaigning for office. Even though I had recently received a newspaper clipping from my father announcing that Washington had just made its first troop reduction, that still left some five hundred thousand of us fighting, and a thousand of us dying every month.

After the singing, stories and such came to an end, us guys were supposed to stay and shovel the fire out and clean up. "Why don't you go ahead Chris, the girls have the flashlights, you'll see much better if you go with them. We can handle this ourselves." "OK Drew, thanks." Then talking to the both of us, "He sprained his ankle, Annie can help you, right Annie?" "Of course I will." I then had to tell Annie what happened while Max pulled me to my feet." As Annie and I started back with the others we quickly fell behind, our light beam dimming from worn batteries; we could no longer be seen. Now close to each other, bouncing our hips off one another from my wobbling, I am now drawn to her even more than before. To feel her at my side, her hand now in mine, I am deliriously content to be with Annie.

In an instant, without a word spoken, we both stopped, turned towards one another and pulled ourselves in even closer. She was pressing against my body like she never wanted to see this night end. Neither of us wanted to release our grip but I had to say, "We should go,

The Kitchen Boys will be along soon." Our hands clasped once again as we continued along the path until we approached the bright spotlights illuminating the girls' cabins. The other campers were still milling around outside before they went in for lights out, so both of us had to drop our hands and part.

Under the lights I could now see her face clearly as she said, "Goodnight Chris, I had a lot of fun, see you tomorrow, sleep well." I think she's talking about my sprained ankle but I'm not feeling anything except an emotional avalanche of all that is good. "Goodnight honey, see you tomorrow." Honey? I don't call anyone honey, it just slipped out, it's how I felt, nothing to apologize for. I went straight to my room, ate some pistachios in bed, thought about all that had happened, and stared at the ceiling for an hour before finally falling asleep.

The next morning the usual group started to congregate on the porch, Annie and I have been coming earlier and earlier each day to try to squeeze in some alone time. "Annie, before anyone else comes I want to tell you about a dream that I had last night." "Hope not about basketball, how's your ankle?" "Much better, I went to work at five-thirty as usual, but anyway, I couldn't tell Bobby or Max about my dream, they'd just laugh at me, which is OK because I never take them seriously. Do you think that dreams have any meaning? I dreamt that after your Playhouse talent show in a couple of weeks I took a walk in the woods with an older white-haired man dressed in a white robe or uniform. He was trying to tell me something but I couldn't understand, he was speaking in German, or something that sounded like that. As he was leading me, paying attention only to him, I accidentally stepped on the head of a large snake. The snake became very angry and demanded that I take my boot off of his head with the promise to let me pass freely. As I lifted my foot I saw not one head, but twelve, a twelve-headed serpent. In an instant he sank his venomous fangs deep into my flesh rendering me prostrate, face down in the dirt, unable to move or speak. That's how I remembered it."

"You think it's silly, don't you?" "No, no, no Chris, let me think. When I was young my father used to interpret dreams for us at home, much of what he said, would happen. I used to call him a 'fortune teller,' but he would turn it around to say that we were telling *him* the story, he was simply repeating it back, using different words. He would tell me that good things would always come from my dreams, but he's not here anymore to help me, he died on my tenth birthday. Maybe I can take his place! I'll be *your* fortune teller," as she forced a smile.

I was quickly losing interest in any interpretation, now I wanted to know more about her father. Finally, "It's nothing Chris, we all have weird dreams." Annie always had a big smile on, but her disposition seemed to have saddened after she mentioned her father. I wanted to understand more about him but decided to ask some other time.

The next day after breakfast I had to set up for lunch at the camp beach. That's what we did twice each camp session. It was another gorgeous sunny day at Shandalee, maybe a bit cool for July, but spectacular nonetheless. "One of the ten best days of the year," I often heard weathermen say. If anybody was actually counting, they probably used that wording maybe twenty or thirty times a year, but everyone still knew it was a beautiful day.

After Annie's swimming lessons were over, I asked her CIT, Ellen, if I could recruit her to help me set up. Ellen was a great girl, all the campers liked her, probably because she was closest to the age of the senior campers like Annie. Ellen and I were always joking about something. We kinda started the first week when she stepped on my toes a couple of times, unintentionally of course. That wouldn't have been so bad except when the other Kitchen Boys and I were off work, we always went barefoot, walking to the beach or just around. Like eating pistachio nuts, it's just something that we did at Shandalee. Within a few days I wound up scraping most of my toes on the asphalt paths within the camp. Worse still, I was swimming in the lake and stepped on an open mussel shell which cut deeply into another of my toes; my feet were killing me so much that I could hardly put on any shoes or sneakers. Ellen felt so badly for stepping on them that she wrote a note and handed it to me one night at The Lodge. It was an apology and promise that she would, "Never come near me again or hurt me in any way." It was hysterical! We laughed and said that I forgave her. Friends ever since.

I saw the two of them, Annie and Ellen that is, talking and nodding their heads, then giggling a bit before Annie came walking towards me from the lake. It was like I was a pubescent kid again seeing the movie "*Dr. No*" for the first time, where Ursula Andress rose from the Jamaican surf wearing a white bikini to confront Sean Connery. I'm thinking how lucky I was that Annie was my friend too, say my best friend, and most unexpectedly, that I was in love. If only we were Honey

Ryder and James Bond, alone on that beach! Ellen knew what was going on and was happy to "volunteer" Annie.

"So Chris, Ellen says you need some help setting up for lunch. You know there are a hundred campers, why did you pick me?" "C'mon Annie, you know why. All the other campers already said no, you're the last one I asked!" "Ha, ha, ha; I'll run up to change, be right back!" "No you're fine like that." "Yeah sure, I don't want the other Kitchen Boys gawking at me. This is only for you alone," then spinning around to make sure I saw *everything*. "Be right back!" "Need any help," I yelled out as she dashed off, everything jiggling and shaking as she disappeared into her cabin.

In a few minutes she was back and joined me in setting up the tables and chairs. "Annie, you know that I want to learn so much more about you and your family, it's just how I feel about you." "Me too, that's important, but I'd like to think that we have a lot of time, we'll just have to make it work. So, what do you want to know? We can take turns, you first." Tell me about your father who passed away on your birthday. What happened?"

"He was the best father anybody could want. He was always a lot of fun around the house and loved his vacations, probably because he didn't take much time off." "Why not, what did he do for work?" "He was a young medic in the Korean War and became a doctor and surgeon after he got home. He loved, absolutely loved his work and he loved Mom and me more than that. His name was Hans. Mom liked to call him, 'My little Hansel,' which always seemed odd to me because he was not a little or small man. He was as tall as you but very large, not fat, just a big guy. I like to say he spoiled mom, me not as much. It was just the three of us. They had helped me plan my birthday party at the house and I invited eight of my friends. It was Saturday, a couple days before my actual birthday. He was going to come home after his rounds at the hospital, he always wanted to be sure that all of his patients were taken care of. You know the hospital down the street from us, a short walk. He was to help Mom with some of the yard games we planned for the afternoon."

"Cloudless and warm, it was a perfect mid-September day, weather pretty much like today, maybe one of the last best weekends for swimming in our pool. After lunch Mom brought out more snacks and soda while we were waiting for Dad to arrive before cake and singing happy birthday. After a little while she called the hospital to ask him if he was still on schedule to be home at three o'clock. She never reached him. Apparently things were happening so fast that the hospital hadn't called us yet. He was in the middle of his rounds when he collapsed in the hallway. A massive heart attack, no chance to save him they said. Crazy, right? In a hospital and nothing could be done." "I'm sorry Annie, I wish I knew you back then." "Maybe not, it feels like I cried for years. The party was over, our neighbor stayed at the house while we drove to the hospital. The girls were all picked up by their parents. My 'fortune teller' was no longer. He was a wonderful father, I wish you could have known him too."

"Mom got re-married two years ago, to another good guy, a widower. He wanted to do the right thing, so he adopted me and I took his last name. He hadn't been blessed with children from his first marriage, so I became his daughter. He's very kind to both of us. They helped each other rebuild their lives, their sadness passed, and now have each other to lean on, they need that. I'm not going to be around forever, in three years I'll be off to college, then med school, it's what I want to do, it's what I have to do."

# Chapter V
# **Sermon on The Great Lawn**

It only took a couple of days before my ankle injury was one hundred percent better and I was really excited about finishing the game that I had to leave prematurely. On the first opportunity that I had to talk to James, I asked him about it. "James, I know we lost to your CYO team because of me. Can you get them back here for a rematch? I think I'm up to it and we stand a very good chance if we practice a little bit more, just saying." "I wasn't going to mention anything to anybody, but I'm not going to lie to you Chris, there isn't going to be another game with the CYO." "You're their coach just tell them they have to, we challenge them!" "Chris, you have to understand that all things are not as simple as you would like to see them. It's not always black and white, but in this case it is, regrettably."

"Listen to me very carefully so you understand. There are campers here at Shandalee who have come with notions of superiority and privilege. Still others claim a disadvantage or handicap because of their color or the social status into which they were born. You know this, you're not so blind or stupid. Even as I am living my life trying to do the right thing all the time, I am up against both sides. The day after our game Miss Ahearn called me into the office to inform me that Shandalee facilities are 'strictly for use by campers and staff.'" "Hey James, I didn't know that was a rule, we, I mean you invited them, that must count for something." "Yes it should, but I know what she meant; don't be bringing your Negro friends up here. I understand that she has a camp to run and lately she's been under a lot of pressure to keep the peace in the cabins. I think she was overreacting to my CYO guys, but I didn't want to push it."

"Look Chris, you're a good guy and I know you'll keep this Ahearn thing confidential, I have bigger issues that I'm facing. I again have to ask you for your unconditional support." "I agree, it was just a friendly basketball game, and that's all it was, good fellowship and fair competition. But what else is going on with you?" "First and foremost, I'm here to make money to add to my savings for college in the fall, that simple. But second, I'm somehow thrust into this position as some kind of mediator here, not something that I sought." "I'm listening James, but I still don't know how I can help." "You know Ruby, right?" "Yeah sure, that cute camper who looks like your little sister." "Well, she's from Paterson too and I know her family, doesn't have a father, so she thinks of me as a surrogate father, and that's fine. She confides in me about important things in her life and one of those 'things' is a developing animosity between the young campers, not so much the older ones."

"Just last week one of Ruby's friends was being sat on and punched by another camper before her counselor could break it up. The irony is that Ruby's friend was the white girl on the bottom and the one provoking the whole thing was a Negro girl. Beth, confirmed the whole thing to me, just like Ruby had said. This isn't the only incident, the one girl was sent home, but we can't send everyone home. I can't send Miss Ahearn home too."

"Chris, all I am asking you to do is be a peacemaker whenever you see something going wrong. You live in New Jersey, you know what I'm talking about. Remember the race riots in Paterson five years ago, they were centered in the ward in which my mother lives. I hated to have her see that. Then the bigger one in Newark just two years ago, practically to the day." Yes, I knew well what James was talking about from when I used to read the newspapers back home. But what could I really do here at camp?

Void of any immediate solutions I had to ask, "What about Miss Ahearn and the counselors, what are they doing?" "Absolutely nothing until the next incident, and then the next, and the next." "Miss Ahearn should address the entire camp, telling them straight, just like you do James." "I'm afraid that she wouldn't be taken seriously by all the campers. Same thing if the counselors tried, as sincere as they might be. The colored girls wouldn't pay any attention to speeches or lectures from them. Part of the problem here is that there isn't a single Negro counselor or CIT at camp. On one hand it's a very good thing that girls of different color share the same cabin, all mixed I mean. Don't worry for now Chris, I'll know what to do." James was absolutely right in all that he was saying now and in the beginning, on our walk to Roscoe. He wasn't kidding when he said, "I promise that we are going to have a very interesting summer at Shandalee."

It had been brutally warm and humid for a week, everyone seemed to move more slowly and the normal friendly patience of *everyone* was being strained. So it wasn't long before another "incident" took place, this time down at the beach. Something stupid about a mix-up in towels between two campers. It should have been nothing, just a misunderstanding or minor disagreement, but because it was between a Negro and white girl it took on a sinister life of its own, it became a racial thing.

By the next morning I knew that something must be up, Miss Ahearn did not make her customary appearance at breakfast, nor at lunch. Even my confidant James was quiet, not revealing anything after I asked about the conspicuous absence of Miss Ahearn. By dinner it was widely known that there was going to be a "mandatory event" on "The Great Lawn" between The Big House and the lake. Just before the end of dinner Miss Ahearn came onto the PA system. We heard her through the speaker in the kitchen and could probably be heard through every speaker at camp. "Good evening everyone, I hope that you enjoyed your dinner on this warm summer evening. I am inviting the entire camp community to attend a special presentation on The Great Lawn tonight at seven o'clock. I expect to see everyone there, staff included. You will not want to miss this." That was it, as she abruptly shut off the PA. There was no "birthday acknowledgement," "saying of the day," "prayer of the day," or some interesting nature "fun fact" that she always liked to interject into her announcements.

Noting Miss Ahearn's serious tone, the entire camp was abuzz with chatter. All speculations of an outdoor movie, sing-a-long or campfire were dismissed, it just didn't feel right. So we waited. Before seven we began to take our seats on the grassy sloping hill, now generally brown from the recent heatwave. Some brought blankets, others pillows to sit on. The cabins had already been emptied, still way too hot inside from the scorching mid-day sun. Some sat to the right and some to the left of the paved path splitting The Great Lawn. The Kitchen Boys sat together. I even saw crotchety Chef sitting in the back on a folding chair that he brought, that's OK, he was there. Everybody was there, except Miss Ahearn and James. The gathering was more toward the lake which perhaps made us all feel a bit cooler.

Then precisely at seven someone noticed Miss Ahearn coming off the porch and then everyone was turning their heads to see. Despite the heat she walked briskly down the path to stand on the beach facing us. In front of her was a small table on which sat her megaphone. Promptly picking it up she began, "Thank you all for coming. I'm sorry that it couldn't be a little cooler this evening. I felt that I needed to address some concerns that you may have had recently, ignoring them would be a grand mistake. I don't pretend to know everything, nobody does, but tonight I thought it best if I invited one of our own to share a personal experience which may cause some of us to think about ourselves and those around us in a different way." Now looking towards the porch in the distance, "James, come on down here please." We turned our heads around once again and sure enough, James, who had been standing in the back came down to the beach to join Miss Ahearn. After being handed the megaphone, "Thank you Miss Ahearn." As she took a seat on the grass with one of the cabins I was prepared for a real barn burner, I wasn't disappointed.

"Since you got here I have shown each of you a great deal of respect, and I suppose that you appreciate that. I have gone out of my way to learn each of your names, not so easy, there are so many of you, and you know mine. I am older than all of you campers, CIT's and Counselors too. I think the only ones older than me are Miss Ahearn and Chef Jones," initiating some restrained laughter. Did you know that's his name, Mr. Jones? He's a person too! The next time you see him why don't you thank him for the meals he prepares for you every day. You like his special pizza, right? Again more applause acknowledging their satisfaction. Does it matter to you that he was born a Negro and half of you are Caucasian? Of course all of you like his pizza, so do I. Does it matter that our dedicated Camp Director Ahearn is white? Many of you girls are only here because of her compassion. I guarantee that *all* of you from my hometown Paterson and *all* of you from Newark are here because she convinced the Camp Board of Directors five years ago that a '*Summer to Share*' program would benefit us all."

"Truly I say to you, every one of us has a lot to be thankful for, know that and remember it every day. Even though we look different, each of us is no better than the person next to us." He then broke his own rule and promise that he had gotten from me and told the entire camp about his great-great-great grandfather, James Parrot and the survival of the Parrot family. I was stunned, there was dead silence as he told his story; not even a sneeze, cough or any other spoken word other than that from James Parrot. It was the most powerful moment that I ever experienced; I was blessed to have witnessed it. "Go now and remember what I said. Be cool." We all watched as he pointed to Miss Ahearn nodding his head in appreciation and smiled briefly.

As he started to walk up the path back to The Big House pockets of people started standing in place and then everyone, clapping and yelling his name, "James," he wasn't "Parrot" anymore. Some of the campers reached out to touch him as he walked slowly past, others were crying, maybe out of guilt, or maybe just because his words were so powerful and had real meaning on this warm July evening in 1969.

Nobody moved from their spot until we saw James go up the porch steps and enter The Big House, the old screen door slapping closed behind him. At this point there was nothing else that Miss Ahearn could have added. I stood and tried to absorb all of the brotherhood that surrounded me; campers, counselors and CIT's crying and hugging each other, it was beautiful. Many lingered with their cabin mates for a long time. This was not the time to be seeking Annie out to fraternize, so I just walked back to The Big House with The Kitchen Boys, each silently reflecting in our own way. I loved James.

# Chapter VI
# Grossinger's

Wow, this was going to be great. Max got John to drive him and us Kitchen Boys, Bobby, Drew and I, to the Grossinger's concert. The only catch was that we had to arrive two hours early, no big deal. Work was done by six-thirty, so we needed to leave right after if we wanted to get to Grossinger's around seven, leaving Max two hours to help setup and *Sackcloth* to take the stage at nine.

Once at Grossinger's we easily found the venue where the concert was going to take place. Even though the resort was sprawling, John seemed to know his way around. "I've been to a lot of concerts here when I was younger, you're really going to like the room." "Honky Tonk Heaven" was the name above the entrance where he let us off. "See you after *Vanilla Fudge's* done, look for my car parked over there," pointing to spots a few yards away. "If you run late I'll wait, no worries. I'm going over to the casino to see if I'm lucky tonight, I'm feeling lucky, I think we're all going to get lucky tonight." "Thanks for helping John, see you later," Max called out to John as he parked the car.

Taking control, Max gave us some instructions, "Let's go in, you guys find seats, don't worry about me, I've gotta check out the stage and talk to their sound people." So we did, and found the place to be different than I expected, not like a theater, more like a huge restaurant and bar, in fact several bars in the back and both sides of the cavernous room. Instead of rows of seats there were hundreds of tables and chairs. Looking around toward the rear, a balcony with many more tables. It was exhilarating to be here! Then, as more people started taking tables within the few minutes since we entered, we grabbed a table too. Most tables up front were already reserved but we had found a nice one about in the middle of the room, by the aisle, just for the three of us. Max wouldn't sit, he had work to do, he was very serious about this and jumped right into it. He was no longer just a Kitchen Boy, at least for tonight. I never saw him move so fast, bounding up onto the stage, running around, grabbing this guy and then another to talk to them about something. I wished that we could have helped him more, but he was clearly in charge, and we knew nothing about these things.

I ordered a Coke, the others too, and settled in, still fascinated by the inner workings of putting on a production of this magnitude. The room was steadily filling up with all kinds of people; hippies, well dressed husbands and wives, older people who may not have known what they were buying tickets to, high school kids, kids on dates and groups of guys and girls. Noticeable was a bunch of hippies as they walked down the center aisle past our table, then stopping, looking for something or somebody. I'm thinking, they must be *Sackcloth*! Spotting Max running around on stage they immediately went directly to him. *Sackcloth* for sure. As the five of them huddled around Max I wondered what they could be talking about. From their gestures it appeared that something was not going as planned.

They were just standing there, anchored to the same spot, then finally moving off to the side of the stage to continue whatever there was to talk about. It seemed like they had no concern about the time, now eight-thirty. Bobby, who was closest to Max and knew the rest of the *Sackcloth* guys from high school and around town, was beginning to get a little bit uncomfortable. "I'm going to see what's happening, somethings wrong, this isn't normal, I've been to his shows before." He left his seat and walked up to the stage near where they were huddled. As Max spotted him, he yelled out something and waved him off.

Now back at the table, Bobby's telling us, "Eli's sick, he can't even talk, well, hardly talk, what a bummer." "OK, OK, who's Eli," I asked. "Just their lead singer, he *is* the band! I think Max's gonna cancel. I've never seen him so pissed." "Which one's Eli," Drew wanted to know, as if it mattered. "The guy in the psychedelic shirt, bell bottoms, and Jimi Hendrix hat. This isn't good, how is it even possible to cancel?" Here we are in this honky tonk and Drew looks like he is silently praying. Confused, I had to ask, "Drew, what are you doing?" "In a minute," and in a minute said, "Praying for my friend, you should too." And so we did, Drew led us, this time out loud. Funny, it now didn't seem so strange that we were praying for Max, that he would find "understanding, discernment and peace" at this moment, those were Drew's words. I've never seen him talk to us like that, he now seemed more like James than our little buddy Drew.

Each of us probably had two more Cokes before the lights dimmed at nine o'clock, the strobe lights and the smoke machine adding to the drama; I didn't know what was happening, what about *Sackcloth*? Their drummer walks on stage, takes his seat at his drum set and starts pounding away in sync with the flashing lights. Then one by one the rest of the band took their positions, then finally Eli. "There's Eli, up front where he belongs," Bobby's claiming, then, "Wait, wait guys, that's not Eli, that's Max, what the hell's going on?" Looking more closely I agreed, "Yeah, Bobby's right, it's Max! He's wearing the same Levi's, tie-dye tee and cowboy boots he came in with. Just the hat's different, he's wearing Eli's hat."

I couldn't believe that was *our* Max, he looked like he belonged up on that stage, like he was born to do this. The second he began that first song I knew that the audience was in for something special. His voice was booming, rich and big and full, the highs the lows, he made it his! By the third chorus, the entire audience was singing as the words were being flashed on the multi-colored kaleidoscope rolling on the back screen;

"THE TIMES WERE HIGH ON HARDSCRABBLE ROAD,

MOST OF US WERE THERE,

BOBBY AND JANIE AND GINA AND ME,

WERE CHUGGING THEM DOWN WITHOUT CARE.

IT'S BEEN THREE LONG YEARS,

SINCE WE GOT TOGETHER,

AND THIS WAS THE PLACE TO BE,

THE MUSIC WAS CRANKED,

THE DRINKS WERE BIG,

AND THE GIRLS GOT IN FOR FREE."

It was shear *Sackcloth* madness in the room, everyone was going crazy. *Vanilla Fudge* was good too, of course. After the concert we found John exactly where he'd said. Soon Max came over to the car, "Can you wait a few more minutes while the band loads the 'chip truck?'" John was the first to ask, "What's a chip truck?" Laughs, "You'll see, it'll only take a few minutes." We all jumped out to help, John too, as Max led us back through the front door, past the stage and through the backstage where there was a swarm of activity, people and equipment all over.

"Hey Max, what's that weird smell." "Not so loud Drew, they're just smoking some joints, grass; can you dig it?" I don't know about Bobby, but this is the first time I've ever smelled it. You could tell that Drew was dumbfounded by the revelation. "It's not my thing either," trying to put him at ease. You don't hear, see or smell much of marijuana back in Ridgewood, but I knew that times were changing fast. We found the band's truck at the loading dock next to *Vanilla Fudge's* monstrous semi.

It turns out that the "chip truck" was an actual chip truck, or at least a former chip truck. That's what the band called it, an old *Charles Chips* box truck that once delivered tins of potato chips and pretzels to homes in the area. I don't know which one of his bandmates owned it but somebody did a horrible job painting over the logo and the rest of the truck too. Looks like they did it with a worn paint roller, terrible, so it was easy to read "Charles Chips" through the half-ass paint job. On the other hand, it's exactly what you would expect for a garage band starting out in 1969.

As we're loading the truck I'm looking around for the *Vanilla Fudge* guys, just because I'm a big fan of theirs too. Soon they appeared and started loading their own stuff. Seeing Max, one of them says, "Great show Max, very groovy. You know *Led Zeppelin* used to open for us, now *Sackcloth*! You're like Robert Plant without the British accent." I'm wondering who's Robert Plant, never heard of him, but Max would know, he knows all about musical things. "Everybody, this is Mark, Tim's over there and Vince and Carmine too. I almost forgot, sorry, this is Mike Lang, taking a break from a local music festival he's working on. And these are my friends who came with me tonight, Bobby, Chris, Drew and John." "Far out Max, far out. You know we gotta be out of here by one o'clock, some kind of Grossinger's rule, see you guys around." It was super cool to be with Max and be part of his music world, if only for one night.

Once back in John's car and on the road to Shandalee, Max thanked us all for coming. Over and over he told us, "Thank you, thank you, thank you. I couldn't have sang without you being here." "Max, are you crying?" "Of course not Bobby, you're an idiot!" We all roared with laughter as he wiped his eyes again. I had no idea that he was so sensitive or didn't understand that we were brothers, partners in crime, even Drew, at least for the rest of the summer.

We were out of control during the short trip home, laughing about everything that happened that night. Spontaneously, Max, still on a high from his performance, led us in singing *Sackcloth's* newest trademark song, certainly the impression we got from the audience reaction tonight. Since Max had written the music and lyrics I could not have been happier for his success.

*"The times were high on Hardscrabble Road,*
*most of us were there, Bobby and Janie and Gina and me,*
*were chugging them down without care.*
*It's been three long years, since we got together,*
*and this was the place to be, the music was cranked,*
*the drinks were big, and the girls got in for free."*

It seemed like Max was on his way up. "One more thing I gotta tell you, maybe you know it already, Mike and I were talking backstage. There's another concert at the end of the summer, not too far from here, an outdoor concert, past Liberty, in Bethel, maybe thirty minutes." "Oh wow, can we all go again, like we did tonight," Drew was bursting. "Don't I wish Drew. It's going to be an entire weekend, probably longer than that for me, Miss Ahearn's never going to let us all go, not all of us." "You've got that right, not *any* of us, not even you, so what are you gonna do Max?" "I don't know Bobby, but I'm going. No pay, just a lot of goodwill for the band." "This is going to be great opportunity for you Max, what you always talked about. I'll do whatever you want to help you with Ahearn." "Me too," added Drew and I agreed.

"So who else is playing?" "That's what I'm trying to say Chris, *Sackcloth* isn't playing, the band is just going to be part of the sound and stage crew, it'll be a lot of work, but worth it." "Once I go I can't come back to The Big House for the last week of camp. I'll have to leave early in the morning and will be staying at my uncle's house, my mother's brother Max, I'm named after him. The concert is being held on his cow farm, it's the perfect place for an outdoor concert, hope the weather is nice!"

Bobby's now dying to know, "Max, you never said, who's playing?" "Are you all ready?" Trying to build on the drama, he finally gives in, "That's right, *The Who,* and *Jimi Hendrix, Grateful Dead, Janis Joplin, Jefferson Airplane*; I forget the rest, but everybody's going to be playing there. Far out, right?" "Unbelievable," even the usually contemplative John was awestruck with Max's apparent rise. "Keep all of this to yourselves until I tell Miss Ahearn, she's going to freak out. I don't know when the best time to tell her would be, I'll figure it out, it's my problem." "Then it will be *our* problem, we'll be short one Kitchen Boy," said Drew, gently protesting. Not wanting to further complicate things for Max I said, "Don't worry, we'll figure this out, worse case, we do it one man short, not a big deal."

# Chapter VII

# Christmas in July

Each session, on the fourth or fifth Wednesday of the month, the camp holds its *Christmas Talent Show* performance, in July this year on the thirtieth, maybe seven o'clock or so. *All* of the campers, CIT's and counselors have to participate, whether designing and painting sets, working the stage, performing solo acts of a special talent or in groups, or in skits they wrote, it was wide open. The counselors from last year had told me that it's a tradition for Miss Ahearn to dress up as Mrs. Santa Claus and randomly hand out the small gifts that the girls had spent weeks making in arts and crafts class.

Normally John would have been in charge of setting up all the microphones and lights for this and any other special camp event. Unfortunately, he'd been called out of town due to an actual family emergency and hadn't returned yet. Miss Ahearn wasn't too upset, she liked John, so she asked Beth to fetch me since I was the one who fixed her office intercom and the camp loudspeaker system a week ago. Frankly it was just dumb luck that I figured it out. She should have summoned Max, the real audio-visual technician. But, hearing her request too, Annie yells out, "I'll get him, where is he?" "Probably up in The Lodge, go run up and find him. The shows going to start in an hour, so get going."

Except for Handyman, we always closed our room doors at any time of day or night, so not surprising to receive a knock from any of The Kitchen Boys before coming in. But, I was a bit startled when I heard the old door hinges creak open, immediately thinking the old drafty hallway was to blame. I had been gazing down at the magnificent lake and the beehive of camp activity surrounding The Playhouse.

Instead, I saw another equally beautiful sight, it was Annie! "Come in, come in quickly, you're not supposed to be here, it's off limits, didn't you see the sign? You should know that. Did anyone see you?" I quietly closed the door and dropped the eye hook to lock it. "No Chris, there wasn't anyone in The Lodge so I came up to find you." I wasn't so worried about myself, but for Annie. The Kitchen Boys always found a way to circumvent most of Miss Ahearn's rules but if caught, the consequences from anyone breaking her primary rule was unthinkable; **"NO GIRLS ALLOWED ON THE SECOND FLOOR!"**

Annie appeared very calm and her ease quickly put my fears of discovery aside. "Sorry, it's nice to see you, I was going to come down for the show in a few minutes and thought we could spend a little time afterward." Taking one step closer to me she whispered, "We have a little time now." Inches now separating us, I could feel the heat from her lithe body, she never looked so inviting. Knowing what was going to happen I had to ask, "Do we need anything?" "No, not for me." My hand went up onto her, her hand went down to me, our lips met and I laid her back onto my mattress. "Are you sure," I whispered. "Yes," and we became one.

I was now beginning to see a *life* together with Annie, it was all so perfect, what did it matter that she had three more years of high school and I had a nearly equal commitment to the Army? Any sadness from knowing that she was going home tomorrow had been offset by these unanticipated minutes together. Whatever it was that I had felt about Annie was now one of absolute devotion. My immediate thoughts were again abruptly interrupted by Annie, "You've got to get down to

The Playhouse right away, Miss Ahearn sent me up here to find you."
"Why me, what does she need?" "I don't know, she said that the
microphones aren't working and you'd know how to fix them." "Yeah,
OK, we better go. All the equipment here is old, about as old as her."
Annie laughed as she got herself dressed and me too. I would now have
to wait for another opportunity to express my feelings, something that I
was getting better at doing, thanks to her.

Hearing nothing in the hallway I unlocked the door, stuck my
head out and told my new love to exit quietly and meet me on the porch.
Before she passed through the door, I kissed her again and quietly said,
"This is a day that I'll never forget Annie." "I feel the same Chris," then
slithered down the hall as I stood watch.

Now both outside, we ran down the path to The Playhouse, only
to find Max with a bunch of wires in his hand explaining something to
Miss Ahearn. Seeing us she said, "What took you so long? After you
left Max walked in and fixed us up for tonight. I think this wiring is as
old as I am," laughing at herself. "No, stop it," I said. Annie could hardly
keep from bursting out laughing too. But it was all good, I never had to
answer Miss Ahearn's question, "What took you so long?" "Chris, did
you know that Max was so talented?" "Miss Ahearn, you couldn't even
imagine how indispensable that Kitchen Boy is around here. He'll be
famous someday." Max, quickly wanting to extract himself from the
conversation, pulled me aside to help him with something. It wasn't
anything to discuss now but reminded me that Miss Ahearn wasn't
going to be so happy with him at the end of August.

By the time the *Christmas Talent Show* started all of us Kitchen Boys were standing in the back, the campers and counselors completely filling the benches. It's always tough to be the first act but the dozen or so counselors came to rock'n'roll. After Miss Ahearn made a few housekeeping remarks on fire exits, bathroom break, and the program she congratulated all of the first session campers for an outstanding four weeks. Then, one by one she acknowledged all of the counselors and CIT's, asking them to stand as the girls hooted and hollered as each stood briefly. It was rather unexpected when she announced her appreciation for all the rest of us; "Gina, John, Gabe and the kitchen staff, thank you," extending the applause; The Kitchen Boys just waved. The only ones mentioned who weren't there included Gina, Gabe, and Chef. I never heard anyone call Handyman, "Gabe," but I knew who she meant.

As she left the stage and disappeared into the darkness off to the side The Playhouse lights were dimmed and the curtain drawn. Once the spotlight illuminated center stage the first performance group was revealed, the opening number! The audience roared with their approval. It was *all* of the counselors, dressed up in funny floppy hats and flowing dresses. Among them was one man, at least dressed up like a man. You could hear the campers echoing each other, "It's Beth, it's Beth, it's Beth!" I'm thinking what a great sport she was and how much I had misjudged her. She's really neat, very cool to do this! Again the cheering was revived as the recorded music gave us the first notes of one of the Top 40 songs playing on the radio that summer; *Sweet Caroline* by *Neil Diamond*. In the counselors' spoof of the hit song, Beth was strutting around the stage serenading the girls and lip syncing the lyrics. But, by the first chorus the entire camp community had joined them in a spirited sing-along. I hated for them to leave the stage, they were so hilarious.

As if it couldn't get any better, a single spotlight then followed Ruby on a slow walk to center stage. She was a tiny thing, maybe thirteen, but tonight she looked like a star six feet tall. She was wearing a psychedelic pantsuit crowned with a magnificent towering Afro wig. There was no lip-syncing for Ruby, instead she belted out her lively rendition of *Diana Ross's* popular song, *Love Child*. This time nobody sang over her performance but watched in amazement as Ruby took complete control of the stage and audience. At the end of her number everyone stood and clapped, maybe her first standing ovation. As they continued to applaud and carry on you could see that she was crying, tears of joy I would hope. Max wasn't the only star at Shandalee!

I had been wondering if it would happen, the act that would be as obvious as anything else, and it did. Beth again turned up the heat in The Playhouse, lip-syncing *Tip Toe Through the Tulips,* wearing a plaid blazer and fake-playing the trademark ukulele likened to *Tiny Tim.* The audience loved it and clearly they loved Beth. After a couple more performers it was time for the gifts to be handed out, which was actually quite orderly and quick. Row by row a hundred or so campers started a processional onto the stage to be handed their gifts by Miss Ahearn, I mean Mrs. Santa Claus. Some lingered a bit longer to hug her, and from the expressions on her face, that was surely the best gift for Miss Ahearn. Upon the return of the campers to their benches, Miss Ahearn,

Beth and the rest of the counselors led everyone in singing *Silent Night* and wrapped it up with *We Wish you a Merry Christmas*.

I knew that Bobby had been drinking before he arrived for the talent show. A telltale sign was his increased perspiration and smell of Listerine mouthwash. The now frequent combination of his *English Leather* cologne, *Southern Comfort*, sweat and mouthwash was rather distinct. Who did he think he was kidding? At this point in the summer Bobby was really beginning to annoy me, who knows how Max put up with him for so long. Ignoring him for now, once outside The Playhouse, I tried to meet up with Annie but since it was now a half hour past the campers' normal lights out I wasn't too hopeful. More than that, this was to be their last night together in the cabin, tomorrow they leave for home and I'm sure they wanted to spend their remaining hours together. As Annie was swept away in the chaos and swarm of girls returning to their cabins all we could share was a frustrated glance and simple, "Good night." Before turning to go she blew me a kiss, to the delight of all the girls walking with her, just giggling away then imitating her blowing me kisses as well, yeah I was embarrassed.

We were almost back to The Lodge when Max noticed Bobby's absence. "I know we all left The Playhouse together, but he must have ducked out along the way, probably took a side trip into the woods to get another drink, I saw how he looked when he walked into the show. I've tried to help him all year, but he seems to be getting worse." "You're a good friend Max, sometimes we can only do so much," what else could I say? We waited in The Lodge, hoping for some of the counselors and CIT's to return after the show. Rowdy cheers erupted as each of them came in. It didn't look like Bobby was going to make an appearance tonight. We stayed up celebrating with the girls until eleven-thirty, way past my bedtime if I was going to make it to work by five-thirty.

Not too long after, I woke to such a ruckus in the hall, like someone was purposely banging into the walls and knocking on all the doors. I knew it was Bobby when I heard the door in the room next to me slam shut. Ten minutes of his fumbling around before it was quiet. When I arrived in the kitchen at five-thirty James was already there, very unusual since my first week as Karl's replacement. Without showing any emotion, James proceeded to tell me about an incident in Cabin C last night.

"I have to speak guardedly because I don't have all the facts yet." "Go on James," as I began to set up the mixer and pull the ingredients. "There was a 'commotion' in Cabin C sometime after lights out, one of the campers claiming that an intruder entered and 'touched her.' Miss Ahearn called the police and then had me woken to see if I could figure it out with her. How would I know anything more than her? Sometimes I think she believes that I know everything, I don't. The police took statements from each of the Cabin C girls and finished up by two o'clock." I have always been known to be judgmental, but like James, I wasn't ready to jump to any conclusions.

I finished baking and then joined The Kitchen Boys to work breakfast. "Bobby, I heard you come in late last night, fumbling around like a fool, what the hell were you doing?" Believing that I had exposed him, his eyes began to well up and was now sobbing. "Come with me," as I pulled him into the food pantry to get some privacy. "I've done a very bad thing Chris and then I made it worse." "Bobby, It's going to be OK if you tell the truth, what happened?" Barely audible, head down in apparent disgust with himself, "I have demons which now control me, demons from my drinking. I blame me, nobody else. After the show I wanted to go to The Lodge with you guys but instead I went into the woods for a night cap."

"After a little too much I went over to Cabin C to see if Janie was still up. Instead of knocking on the door which would have also been incredibly stupid, I opened the door and went over to her bunk, the one next to the door, just to say goodnight. That's when I nudged her arm, only to find that she had traded the upper bunk for the lower. All of a sudden the girl in the upper bunk started screaming and then all seven campers started screaming. I am so sorry! The counselor on duty in the cabin, I think it was Kirsten, started yelling and chased me out and into the woods where I lost her. I picked the wrong bunk, I'm so stupid."

"When the screaming first started I looked down and saw Janie on the bottom bunk. I don't think she even knew it was me, it was so dark and she probably couldn't see my face from down there, I don't know. After waiting in the woods a while I came back to The Big House, you heard me come in." "Yes, I heard you, and probably everyone else!" "The first thing this morning Miss Ahearn was in the kitchen to share the basics of what happened, then she pulled each of us aside to see what we knew." "Bobby, this is not the end of the world, the mistaken identity I mean. Your 'demons' are far more serious. What else aren't you telling me, you said, 'then I made it worse.'" "The one girl whose arm I nudged couldn't identify me, but another girl in the cabin said that it could have been Handyman, now it's all over camp about Handyman. Miss Ahearn didn't tell me anything really, just the basics. I can't even be relied upon to tell the truth any longer, it's that bad."

Despite the recent lows triggered by Bobby and spectacular highs with Annie all month, the last day of the July session had arrived, something that I hoped would never come. For a week or more I struggled for the words I could use the morning when all campers were to pack up and move out, back to their homes. What I didn't know about the last day, until I arrived for my breakfast shift, was that the campers would be departing *immediately after* breakfast. The buses were to pick them up at The Big House, in front of the porch where it all began for Annie and I.

Because all of us Kitchen Boys had continuous duty beginning at the start of meals, through the meals and ending about an hour after the meals, I was rather worried that I would be missing the campers' departure; that really means Annie's departure. It was killing me to be racking all the dirty glasses into the dishwasher, knowing that the little remaining time with Annie was ticking away. As soon as I thought that I was finished with my kitchen chores I asked James if I could be dismissed so that I could get outside. He knew what I was up to, but instead of teasing me, he just said, "Sure." In that instant, I ran out of the kitchen towards the dining room.

As I swung the screen door open and stepped onto the porch I got my first look at all the craziness surrounding the last day of camp. I was told it would be chaotic but this was unbelievable. I didn't see Annie on my side of the three huge chartered buses parked end-to-end so I tried to look on the other side through the narrow spaces between them. Leaving little room between the buses and the porch, most of the good-byes were being said on The Great Lawn down along the line of cabins and extending to The Playhouse by the lake. Along with many smiles, there was an equal amount of crying going on. It would not be easy for some to say goodbye to the new friends they had made at Shandalee. Most would not know when they would see each other again, maybe never, *probably* never. But maybe next year at camp or maybe at the *Shandalee Winter Reunion* in Ridgewood, at least that's what they were promising.

Already behind schedule, the bus drivers were working hard stuffing all of the campers' luggage through the opened compartment doors. There were so many loose items, not packed in suitcases or boxes, making it extremely difficult to load, and probably worse to unload, and then identify. The buses were marked with cardboard signs displaying numbers 1, 2 and 3, so that luggage being stowed would match the campers assigned to that bus, hope that worked out. Those buses would soon form a caravan back to the Ridgewood UCWA, where the campers would find their parents or rides to their homes.

Adding to the chaos were a dozen family cars to pick up their own campers, not choosing to have them return via the buses. The cars were scattered everywhere, blocking the buses from the front and back, and as I walked between the buses, I saw more family cars blocking any way out for the buses. Some of the campers were saying goodbye to me, that's very nice, but I was only looking for one, Annie.

It had already been ten minutes since I had come outside, and still she was nowhere to be found. Then she appeared. She was running toward me, in and around everyone and everything else in her way. She had the biggest smile to greet me. It no longer mattered what I was going to say or how I should act. This emotion was real, not pretend; I was over-joyed to see her too. As she neared, maybe a few feet away, she leaped up into my outstretched arms. It was surprising that she didn't knock me over, there was a lot of power and force generated from that teenage body. As her slender legs were locked around my waist I was being treated to the best bear hug ever.

We knew that we had no time for pretty speeches, promises or cute or funny things to say, we had already done that during our time together at Shandalee. She simply said, "Goodbye my dear friend," and then quickly added, "I love you." I could have said a hundred other things, in fact, common sense would have demanded that I say something else, *anything* else, but without hesitation it just popped out. "I love you too Annie." Then, very naturally, not awkward in any way or emotion, our lips met for the very last time at Shandalee and we kissed. Not a peck on the cheek like you would give some old great aunt that you barely know, but a full lip lock in front of a hundred witnesses. Not at all like the kiss from Gina, this one I wanted and this time I let her in. I didn't expect it to happen that way, but it did. Since we first met I had always tried to exercise discretion in public, even though I had romanticized about Annie practically every time I saw her. Ours was a kiss for all of time, it was real, and more important, it meant everything to us. Then we both knew she had to go.

As I was released she remained silently standing before me. We hugged once again, and then at the same time, which was typical of the way we were both thinking of the same thing we said, "Don't forget to write me," we both laughed.

Miss Muller had already made one announcement over the PA system asking the campers to board the buses. The loudspeaker on the porch was unusually loud today, almost too harsh as it signaled the end to a wondrous and sometimes bizarre first session in that summer of 1969. As she re-emerged from her office toting her megaphone, she was able to thank a few of the parents and allow some of the campers, with whom she had bonded, to show their affection. Then came her second request to board, "Please board your bus, parents you'll have to move your cars once the children are boarded. Thank you everybody, hope to see you again next year."

Unlike our first meeting on the porch, it wasn't just me, we were now *both* unable to move, speak or take a step away, frozen in time. It was especially hard for me to maintain my smile when Annie finally, slowly, took a few steps backwards, also unwilling to fully break the grip that held us. She looked like she had just lost her best friend, I know I had. Then came a flicker of a smile before she turned and slowly boarded her bus. All I could muster was a few waves, not even knowing if she could see me through the darkly tinted windows. "Remember me," I whispered, knowing she could no longer hear me. Then she was gone.

Despite my own selfishness to be losing her for the remainder of the summer I was happy that she would be re-united with her parents. If they only knew what took place during those four weeks that we were together. And to think, the reason they sent her to a Christian girls' camp in the Catskills was to keep her "away from boys," that's what she had told me when we first met. I also had parents waiting to see me, but that wouldn't happen for another month.

As the caravan disappeared down Hardscrabble Road I started walking up to my room for some quiet time. I was still on kitchen duty for the rest of the day but because the campers had left, the kitchen was essentially closed. John had arranged to have lunch and dinner brought up from Tony's Tavern, sandwiches for lunch and then pizza for the Shandalee staff's dinner. From the hallway in front of my room I could hear Bobby in his room. Even though his door was shut I could hear him sobbing, not just crying a little, but full out uncontrollable wailing. Bobby was the last person that I wanted to deal with right now but determined that I best get right to it, picking up where we left off two hours before.

I didn't even knock, I just opened his door. Because I wasn't willing to give him any additional comfort or facilitate his dependencies I just let him have it! "Stop crying and listen to me. Yeah, you've done a very bad thing, especially about Gabriel, you know, Handyman. You should have confessed to Miss Ahearn right at that moment instead of leaving Gabriel out to hang, you lying sack of shit. I tell you now that I will defend Gabriel's name, it's not possible that he assaulted those girls, Bobby, it's simply not possible. He was already in bed sleeping when I came up last night, I saw him. His door had swung open or he forgot to close it. I saw him, and I closed it. There's no reason for him to be sniffing around the girls' cabins." "That's why I'm really in trouble Chris. I told Miss Ahearn that I had seen him wandering around in that area after the show. What's wrong with me Chris?" "Oh my God, you didn't, I think you're sick. You need to get some professional help, but first things first. What was Miss Ahearn's reaction to your disclosure?" "It's like the color drained out of her face, she thanked me and immediately left the kitchen."

# Chapter VIII
# Handyman's Redemption

"Handyman," that's what they called him, the guy who fixed everything at Camp Shandalee. He was the resident plumber, painter electrician, carpenter, grass cutter and permanent resident caretaker when camp was not in season. "Handyman," a name more like a thing rather than a real person. He was really rough looking, not tough looking, just rough! Since he lived in The Big House with the rest of The Kitchen Boys, I saw him nearly every day when he was awake in his room, or just around the camp working. His door was sometimes open, I think mainly to air it out because it smelled like stale pizza and beer, or something like that, or maybe he was just looking for a friend who might happen to walk by. A couple of days after my arrival I had stopped by his room, mainly because I had to walk past it to get to mine. Already late, the rest of us had spent the night in The Lodge doing what we did mostly every night; talking, listening to records, raiding the kitchen for some potato chips and *Cheez Doodles*, and  most important, creating friendships.

He never socialized with any of us, he seemed to be so different than anyone else, and not in a positive way. Yet, there he was, lying on top of his bed, in his pale blue boxers, looking every part of a middle-aged bum. But, a bum reading a big fat book, *Moby Dick*? Something was wrong with this picture. I didn't see any other of us open a book since we arrived at camp. We never even made time to watch TV shows like *Rowan & Martin's Laugh In* or *Hawaii Five-O*, two of my former favorites, and God forbid that we watched the news to keep us informed of happenings outside Shandalee.

Curious about what I was seeing, I stopped at his doorway and said, "Hi, my name's Chris, just wanted to…" He looked up from his book, "I know, nice to meet you, come on in." I don't think that anybody ever went into *his* room. Once a week residents of The Big House could go down to the laundry room and exchange sheets and towels for clean ones. I did, but not sure about anybody else. In the case of Handyman, his lack of any sheets on his bed led me to think that he just skipped the whole thing, now lying on an old stained mattress. There was nowhere to sit so I just took another step in and stood there. After a little bit of small talk I asked him if he liked being called "Handyman." He didn't answer except to say, "Gabriel, my oldest and dearest friends still call me Gabe, these days I like Gabriel." So I called him Gabriel from then on.

I concluded that he was an alcoholic, the smell of whiskey and body odor in his room was overpowering. Already too close, the stink from the dozens of cigarette butts in the ashtray on his nightstand was enough to gag me. Looking more closely, I could see that it was actually an old hub cap. Noticing that I was studying it, "Like it Chris? It's from a 1940 Studebaker Commander. I bought it new, the year after I was married, we had a lot of good times in that car and now all that remains is the hubcap." What could I say? So I said nothing. At times I am a compassionate person, but I couldn't understand why Miss Ahearn would tolerate him; for one thing, his smoking in bed could burn The Big House to the ground. Yet, I never saw his shortcomings interfere with his work at Shandalee, always moving about and getting stuff done.

As I left his room I kept thinking how this man, any man, could let this happen to himself.

It was hard to believe that things had gone so wrong. My friend Bobby had created a problem where one didn't exist. If he had simply told the truth at the time, what could have been viewed as the misguided attempt at romance by a stupid teenager now involved the police making several trips to Shandalee, specifically to interview Gabriel. What could have been handled through the immediate firing of Bobby, had escalated into the harassment of a reclusive man who preferred to be left alone. That's the way I saw the whole thing and that's what I thought of Gabriel. Yet, at the same time, I was sure that the detectives would quickly finish their report and find no reliable witnesses within the dark cabin. Bobby's claim putting Gabriel at the scene was probably irrelevant since practically *all* of the other staff passed Cabin C after the show, hardly making them suspects, and none other corroborating Bobby's claim. I shouldn't have been so sure of everything.

During breakfast shift, one week to the day after the *Christmas in July Talent Show*, Max and I learned from Bobby that Gabriel was going to be charged with sexual assault. However he found out, Bobby shouldn't have been talking about such things to Max and I. It didn't matter if his father or one of the detectives told him, it was wrong to tell us. Upon hearing, it felt like my head was going to explode, I was so pissed at Bobby, I couldn't even look at him, he didn't even seem to care about the trouble he was causing. "Bobby, I'm telling Miss Ahearn everything, I never should have tried to protect you." "I never asked you to protect me, I can take care of myself. What's the difference, he's a degenerate anyway, nobody's gonna miss him." "What are you talking about? Did you consider his reputation, the little bit that you left him? It will be destroyed. Do you want him to die in prison?" Bobby didn't seem interested in responding, instead just smirked. I was furious, I couldn't get away from him fast enough. I wanted to choke him. "I'm seeing Miss Ahearn right after breakfast, I mean it!" Max, who had been silent the whole time just uttered, "My God Bobby, what have you done?"

Today was my turn to roll the oversized garbage bin up to the pen. Normally I didn't mind doing garbage duty, but today I was on a mission to see Miss Ahearn and turn Bobby in. He had let the whole thing get out of hand. I got the kitchen garbage together as quickly as I could and made my way up there. I could see that the raccoons had been out the night before as there were scraps of food strewn around; chicken bones, egg shells and potato skins mostly. I don't know how they did it but I figured that they were simply climbing the chain link fence and opening the bin lids. I took care of the mess by using the snow shovel and broom left there for such a purpose.

Around the back of the pen, near the woods, was a water hose and cans of disinfectant to drizzle onto the pen's concrete pad for a wash-down. It was the only way to keep the odor and cockroaches to a minimum. As I was still following the path of scattered garbage around to the back I saw Gabriel sitting up against a tree, sleeping. As I got closer I could see a small amount of blood coming out the side of his mouth. He looked absolutely terrible. I gently tapped his shoulder to awaken him, "Gabriel, Gabriel." He just fell to his side and lay still. I had never seen a dead person but Gabriel was clearly dead.

I felt his forehead with the back of my hand, really cold, he was dead. His demons would no longer hurt him. Next to him lay an empty pint of *Four Roses* whiskey and a small caliber pistol. It was an ugly scene. I wished that I could fix this for him, nobody should be seen like this. No, there wasn't much self-respect remaining in him, there was nothing left of him except a cold body. All I could do for him now was to prop him back up against the tree. I didn't touch the pistol or bottle, or anything else, just went straight to Miss Ahearn's office.

Running through the kitchen, then dining room, and into the office past Gina I found Miss Ahearn working at her desk. I shut her door. "Gabriel's dead, I just found him up at the pen!" She looked up, just staring at me as if she was trying to process the news just delivered. Not believing her ears, "What did you say?" Again I said, "Gabriel's dead!" I watched as a tremendous strain came over her face, her eyes closed tightly, her fists now clenched, slamming them on her desk, and finally slumping out of her chair onto the floor crying out, "No, no, no, no, no, no, no, not Gabe." I didn't know what to do, so I also dropped to the floor and tried to console her.

Easily hearing the clamor, Gina burst in, "What happened Chris?" "Gabriel has died." "Oh my God, I'm so sorry Miss Ahearn." As Gina bent over to embrace her I got up and with Gina's help managed to pull Miss Ahearn back into her chair. She was out of control, still denying the reality of the news, "No, no, no, no," she repeated over and over. It took a while before she could utter a few words through the torrent of tears. "How Chris." "Gunshot wound Miss Ahearn." "I'm sorry to tell you this. You must have been really close to him." Sobbing, "Close? I loved him. Gabe was once my husband," and then she really lost it, just wailing uncontrollably. I could barely watch this poor woman's suffering. "Gina, are you OK here, I'll find the nurse, think we need her."

The nurse came and sedated Miss Ahearn, and stayed with her, along with Gina. Wasting no time, I took matters into my own hands, sat down at Gina's desk and called the police, first, to tell them of the deceased and second, to reveal the truth about Bobby. Very fast, within minutes, the EMT's and detectives arrived and met me at the porch. I walked them back to the pen, to Gabriel. I told one of the detectives the truth about the night of the assault. He took notes and said that he would probably need to speak with me again. The EMT's just shook their heads when they checked on Gabriel. "Looks like a suicide, happened a while ago," I heard one of them say. The detectives took pictures, asking me to stand back as they finished bagging the gun, bottle and some other stuff for evidence. "Do you know who's the next of kin?" "I think maybe Miss Ahearn here, Camp Director Ahearn. She's probably still in her office with the camp nurse. Let me know where you're taking him so I can tell her." "And who are you?" "I'm Chris Bronson." "How are you affiliated with the camp?" "I'm a kitchen boy."

"Where's Bobby now, another detective asked." "Probably in his room, I'll show you the way." "No, just point me in the right direction, I'll take it from here." Now alone, I waited on the porch to see if I could help Miss Ahearn in some way or if the detectives needed anything else from me this morning. John, who had been returning from two days family leave, came driving up to the porch. "Everything all right at home John?" "Yes, thanks, my mother had gone in for some minor surgery, she's fine now." "John, listen to me, something bad has happened." After giving him only a few details he hurried off to Miss Ahearn. It's true that John was officially the camp's second in charge, under Miss Ahearn, but it was gratifying see his genuine concern for her.

As I waited on the porch, considering the next thing to be taken care of, I saw Bobby within a few yards being escorted to the nearby patrol car. He was crying, but turned to me to say, "I'm sorry Chris." Disgusted by his betrayal of all of us, the most I could offer was, "Good luck Bobby." A trail of dust followed the police car down Hardscrabble Road.

I'm glad that most of the campers and staff were down at the lake for their scheduled morning activities; swimming lessons, water safety and even sailing lessons. They didn't need to see what was going on up the hill. But that also meant that Drew was probably down at the lake enjoying what started off as a splendid summery day. I walked down to look for him and tell him about his Aunt Sue, he was easy to find, sitting alone on the shore trying his hand at fishing. Calling out to him from the beach to join me, "Drew, c'mon over I have something to tell you." Once again I had to deliver the bad news that morning. Clearly shaken, he dropped everything he was holding and raced up the hill to The Big House. Gabriel was his uncle, not any easy thing to tell someone. I picked his stuff up and carried it to his room. My heart was bleeding for Miss Ahearn and for her nephew Drew too, the guy who had been such a pain-in-the-ass the first weeks here. Not at all what I felt about him now.

We didn't see Miss Ahearn for a week following the passing of Gabriel. Indeed she was his next of kin and took care of all the burial arrangements back in New Jersey. It turns out they had no children during the ten years that they were married, and neither did ever wed again. Funny how things aren't always as they appear. During the absence of Miss Ahearn, John took over the Camp Director's duties without any hoopla, a very calming week actually. No surprise, Bobby was fired in a letter that John sent off to his home, and many of us thought that would be the end of it, the police would take care of the rest.

Within a day of Miss Ahearn's return, she received a call from the Livingston Manor Sheriff's office, from Bobby's father! We would never know what was spoken, but that night Miss Ahearn called a staff meeting in The Lodge to give us an update, or as she said, "Before you read about it the local newspaper tomorrow." Even though her eyes were still red from her tumultuous week, there were no tears from her today. She was back! I'm not sure she had any tears left, maybe having shed them all since she first heard the shocking news from me.

"Can I have your attention everyone? You know most of the story surrounding Bobby. I got a call from the sheriff today informing me that Bobby has confessed," then a very long pause. Sure, we kind of thought that he'd already admitted to the charges stemming from Cabin C. But there was something else! Miss Ahearn was stone-faced, dead serious as she made eye contact with each of us, like she was trying to prepare us for what was coming next. "He confessed, to killing Gabe."

We were stunned, unable to speak, then a few murmuring, "No way" and, "It couldn't be." Miss Ahearn agreed, "I wish that it were not true, but the police lab tests confirmed that only Bobby's finger prints were on the bottle and on the pistol, and Gabe's alcohol-blood level was zero." Max just dropped his head, shaking it from side to side, saying nothing, but surely contemplating the fate of his high school friend. I can't conceive of the kind of power that a demon could have had over Bobby, to justify murder, to cover-up an ill-conceived visit to his girlfriend's cabin?

"I know it's hard for us all here. The sheriff told me that Bobby has a lawyer and will plead temporary insanity, to the charge of first degree murder." We were all crushed, devastated with this news. How could we go on for the rest of the session? Like reading my mind, Miss Ahearn closed by saying, "We will go on, we all have a job to do here, and as long as I am breathing, I intend to fulfill the mission of Camp Shandalee, '*Never Alone, Together We Grow.*' I hope you understand if I get back to my office, I have a lot of catching up to do." Now we were the ones shedding the tears as we surrounded Miss Ahearn; I had never before seen this kind of strength in a woman, or any man. She just smiled, thanked us and left the room.

None of us knew what to do, we just stood there without speaking. Then we heard from James, "The Bible tells us, 'Let not your heart be troubled.' Please join me in prayer for our friend Bobby, surely he has sinned but we pray for his repentance and God's forgiveness.

Let's form a circle." All of us there, about twenty, held hands and bowed our heads as James led us in prayer over Bobby and then for Gabriel.

Then James delivered some astonishing news, "Gabe was a great man with a great problem. He squandered practically everything in his life and his weaknesses were well known to many of us who knew him. But what you did not see was how he was recently led to God. I had been talking to him since camp opened in July, just me and him, privately, mostly in prayer. We had just started going to church together, I can tell you that now. I was with him when he went to give confession at Saint Aloysius in town. I tell you, he was changed! Gabe was our brother too, no matter what he had done. I tell you, he is now with God in heaven." He then led us in singing *Amazing Grace*. Yes, truly amazing. James Parrot showed everyone the meaning of repentance, forgiveness and redemption. Even at that moment, I was thinking that I would never again in my life experience the close spiritual connection that had just taken place; it was that powerful.

Later, Max called Bobby's house to see how he was doing. Things weren't good, his father had resigned as Livingston Manor Sheriff to devote all of his time to his son saying, "That's the least that I can do for him, I hope it's not too late." Sadly, the house that Bobby grew up in was now for sale to get money to pay his lawyers. The only positive thing, if you could call it that, was that Bobby's father was going to be staying at his ex-wife's house in town while they tried to help their son through this.

 Chapter IX

# Letters

Everything had changed after Annie went home. I had just spent the best month of my life. I can't compare falling in love for the first time with anything else I have done or may do in the future. But so much of that had to do with Shandalee. It goes without saying, people fall in love every day, anywhere around the world, no matter in what country, no matter what city, town or village. They meet in schools, at work, church, taverns, clubs or on buses or trains I suppose. Shandalee is where we met.

Everyone has a special story of their first meeting. Sometimes it takes weeks or even years for two people to recognize what should have been obvious from the beginning. I never understood how it could take people so much time. I've heard some guys say, "I didn't like her at first, but then she grew on me." Yet, how can it be possible for someone to instantly know? That doesn't sound logical either. But, I am convinced that it is not about logic or some well-quoted formula, like "opposites attract," which wasn't the case between Annie and I.

I remember every word she ever said to me while together at Shandalee, and where we were, the aroma in the air, from the pungent boxwood shrubs around the porch of The Big House to the sweet smelling lily-of-the-valley down at The Playhouse. I remember what Annie wore and more than anything else, how she made me feel. That feeling stayed, but the anticipation from catching the next glimpse of her was gone. Just last week I could always see her at breakfast, lunch and dinner and any other opportunity when we could plot some time together.

To me, everything after Bobby's arrest and departure from Shandalee represented my newer reality, not anything that smelled pretty or was lovely; it was harsh. I likened his story to one of another man's self-destructive nature. If Bobby was Captain Ahab, and his white whale was the demon alcohol he could no longer control or squash, then his last voyage was that of Shandalee, which might make me Ishmael, the reluctant observer in Herman Melville's novel, *Moby Dick*. Like Ishmael, I was a witness to a man's self-destruction, yet I took no substantive steps to help my friend, until it was too late. I regret that deeply. So what or who did that make Gabriel? Perhaps like Queequeg, the Polynesian harpooner, Gabriel was the loner who could be a good friend if given the opportunity, and loyal, to a fault, to those surrounding him. Only in the end was Queequeg able to see the Pequod's downward spiral in which he was caught, and despite it all, was able to find an inner peace, perhaps much like Gabriel.

The first week without her was so crazy here, Gabriel's death and then Bobby's confession, that I tried to focus more on she and me than them and me. True that we were now one short in the kitchen, but James picked up the slack to help, washing dishes and even pots, and taking his turn at garbage duty. James was terrific and always offered me words of encouragement when I was getting hammered in the kitchen or feeling overwhelmed, "Continue your good works and you shall be rewarded a thousand times over." Our problem with manpower was nothing compared to what Bobby was facing. I still had plenty of time to write Annie, but it was from her that I got the first letter; she probably wrote it on the way home, I got it that fast.

Dear Chris,

I'm so sad that I had to leave Shandalee and especially you. My parents thought that I was kidding when I had asked them to stay the August session. Think they just wanted me to be at home with them! I'm a little excited that they surprised me with news of a family vacation down at the Jersey shore before school starts, but I wish that you could be there with us. You know how much I like the shore. I bought you a comb and have it enclosed. You'll need it, your hair was already getting pretty long or you can risk going into town to find a barber. My mother saw the comb after I brought it home and asked why I needed a black comb, a man's black comb. I told her that they use them for crafts at Shandalee, making the bead bracelets. I didn't even know what I was saying but she believed me. Sorry I lied, but better that I don't tell her that I just spent the best month ever with a boy that I am madly in love with. I'll write again soon, enjoy the comb and try not to flirt with any of the other girls.

Love Always,
Annie

I was never one for mushy stuff, but her letter was uplifting and an honest confirmation that what we had was real and would continue. Flirt? No, I didn't want any other girl, I wanted Annie. Although sleepy, I wrote mostly at night as I tried to recuperate from the nine hour kitchen days which were beginning to take a toll on me. Annie was no longer here to get my adrenaline flowing, so I relied on her letters, even those sent from the shore.

Dear Chris,

We drove down to the shore today and traffic on the Garden State Parkway was almost unbearable. My parents are saying that I seem different since I got home, that I'm smiling and singing all the time. That's because of you! You know that I am always cheerful anyway, and consider myself blessed for the things that have been given to me and the people that come into my life. You're one of them. I'll have to tell you about my special grandmother when you get home, I loved her so much. She got married when she was 15. My grandfather used to be a coal miner! When I was young we used to visit their farm in West Virginia for a week every summer. We had so much fun there. We stopped going after my father died, things changed so much, they were his parents. Oh, big news, I got a part-time job at Petite's in Ridgewood, starting as soon as we get back from the shore. I'll be working two nights and

Saturday selling clothes, but really doing anything they need me to do. I'll probably spend all my money there! I got your letter today and feel the same way, I can't wait to hold you in my arms again!

Love Always,
Annie xxooxo

Her letters kept coming, one more lovely than the next, to the point where I thought about driving to see her after my dinner shift and coming back by five-thirty. But, I know that there could be a lot that happens between here and there, preventing my timely return. It was my duty to stay here and that is what I had to do, as much as I was being pulled to go. The words about her grandmother stuck with me every day, "She got married when she was fifteen." I knew what she was saying, not talking about us getting married now, not at all. It meant that she considered herself more of a woman than a fifteen year old school girl, and that's the way I thought of her and the way I treated her.

**Dear Annie,**

*I look forward to getting your letters each day. It's not the same without you but the kitchen is keeping me really busy. James has helped me more than I ever expected, now coming in with me at five-thirty. He doesn't have to do that, but he does anyway. Did you know that he is really religious? He now leads us in silent prayer before every meal. I asked him about that yesterday during baking and he explained it to me in this way. I have received many gifts from God. Through him all things are possible to those that believe, I think he said. He even taught me how to pray, so I tried last night before bed. When I woke up this morning I was unusually happy for some reason, like I was seeing everything in a different way. Even Miss Ahearn said I was joyous this morning when she saw me. "Joyous" she said! I'm starting to believe that prayer works, but not sure if that alone makes me a believer in the way that James said it. I'll have to ask him tomorrow. Sorry to babble on about this but was praying for you and I too. Let me know what's happening in Ridgewood.*

*I LOVE YOU,*
*Chris*

Just like every morning since I replaced Karl the baker, while the entire camp slept, I'm showered, dressed and down to start work at five-thirty. But on this one particular morning, the second Sunday in August, the peaceful quiet of Shandalee was broken by some minor disturbance in front of The Big House. Curious, from the kitchen I walked through the dining hall to discover the old Chip Truck and Max climbing into the passenger seat. I was totally confused about what I was seeing. "Max, what's happening?" "Shh, quiet Chris, I'm leaving today." "What? Leaving for where? Are you coming back tonight?" "No, I got a call from Mike Lang yesterday, you met him at Grossinger's, remember? He said that he needed me and my crew out in

Bethel right away to help set up the stage and sound equipment for the show, the one he's putting on next weekend." "Yeah, you told us about it, but I also remember well that you said it was the *last* weekend in August.

What did Miss Ahearn say when you told her?" "I didn't, there wasn't enough time." "You're screwed, she'll fire you!" Still not believing this was happening I had to ask, "When will you be back?" "I won't, breaking down the stage and sound towers will take weeks, that's what Mike said. Chris, this is going to be a huge event, Mike's saying that they've sold over seventy thousand tickets! I can't pass this up for anything, this is my passion, just like you have yours. Don't hate me, I know that you'll never be able to keep up in the kitchen, but maybe Miss Ahearn can hire somebody for the rest of the session." "That's really crazy talk Max, she wouldn't do it, you know that. Look, we've managed before, don't worry, just go, we'll be OK." "I want to ask you to do one last thing for me Chris, you've treated me like a brother since we met, so I feel that I can ask." "Let's hear it first before I agree." "Try to explain the whole thing to Miss Ahearn this morning before she finds out on her own. After all the poor woman has been through this year I hate to pile this on too!" "OK Max, I'll do my best." "I really gotta go now, take care of yourself Chris and thanks." That was the last I saw Max that summer.

I was truly happy for my friend, he was a good guy and deserved a break. When James popped into the kitchen to check on me I told him *everything*, beginning with the Grossinger's concert where we first learned that Max would be taking time off. He wasn't happy, said he wished that Max had told him earlier, but he understood his motives, explaining, "Look Chris, I've been working hard for a lot of years to get to college, I'll be the first in my family. There's nothing of this earth that can stop me now, same thing for Max, neither one of us nor our Miss Ahearn could have changed his mind. So, it looks like it's going to be Drew, you and me for the next three weeks. Ya know, I'm going to talk to Warren to see how he can help too. And one more thing, because you knew about this since your trip back from Grossinger's, I'm going to stick you with informing Miss Ahearn. Why don't you go now, you're almost done, I'll take the rest of the rolls out of the oven."

"OK James, that's fair."

I would have put off telling her the bad news till later but since Miss Ahearn could walk into the kitchen at any time, and James was instructing me to do it right now, I took off my baker's apron and headed over to her office. "Hi Gina, is Miss Ahearn in?" I was hoping for, "Not yet," but I got, "Morning Chris, yes, go right on in, knock before you enter." I knocked and found her deep into some kind of accounting work, her fingers flying over her electric adding machine, clearly busy. "Hi Chris, how are you this morning?" "Been busy but have to tell you that Max quit this morning and won't be coming back." There, I got it out in one breath, I didn't plan it, it just came to my mind that he in fact quit, abandoned his job, so no use to upset Miss Ahearn with having to go through the motions to fire him.

"Oh no, that's strange and not like him at all, what happened?" "He got another summer job with some concert show, setting up the stage and whatever else he's been doing with his band." "I wish him luck, now I expect you and James and my nephew to fill in the gap, figure it out and let me know what you decide. Maybe Warren or John can help, I'm going to leave it up to you. Sorry they left you to tell me, you'll be fine!" "Will do Miss Ahearn." As I walked out of her office I'm thinking that's one cool cat, she wasn't bummed, just took it in stride. What a difference since I delivered the news of Gabriel's death, she's truly back!

Even while it was happening we heard all about the Woodstock Music and Arts Festival, at Yasgur's farm, Max Yasgur's farm. I guess that Mike Lang, the promoter we met at the *Vanilla Fudge* concert, underestimated a little bit. He told Max that over seventy thousand people might show up, they are now saying five hundred thousand! We were near Bethel so it was in all the local papers and on the radio. Something over a half million people showed up, maybe more. This was so cool for Max. Though all of us talked about going for a day there was no chance that anyone else left in the kitchen could leave Shandalee, and that was OK too. I heard that Sherry and one of the other CIT's said that they were going "just for the day." I guess they did, but forgot to come back, too much fun, sounded like it. Go Sherry!

I struggled through the last two weeks of camp, fulfilling all of my kitchen obligations as I contemplated my immediate future. Instead of appearing in The Lodge every night I limited it to weekends. The rest of my evenings were spent writing to Annie and reading books that James and I had picked up on a second trip to Roscoe. Suddenly the summer of 1969 was over, saying goodbye to everyone was the second saddest day of my life, saying goodbye to Annie had been sadder.

# Chapter X
# Saying Goodbye to Annie Again

Despite the fact that I was so mixed up about the "movie date" with Sally, by unwittingly suggesting that we go to the movies, she later thought the whole thing hilarious after I confessed that I had been avoiding her for a couple of weeks. It further proved my belief that girls are simply more mature than us guys. As she explained, "Soon as Miss Ahearn confirmed the day and time of the scheduled moon walk we made plans to set up a couple of televisions at The Playhouse for a *'Moon Walk Slumber Party.'* Sorry no boys invited! I thought it would eventually occur to you that there was a conflict. The Manor Theater was even closed that evening."

What a good sport she was about the movie date cancelation, really my fault as I had let my imagination get the best of me. Since Sally didn't have her own car I was happy to offer her a ride home in my Nova. She also lived in Ridgewood, as did several other counselors, which made sense since all of us were hired through the UCWA facility in town, also recruiting from Livingston Manor; students at Manor High, like Max, Bobby, and Sherry too. Except for the first hour, neither of us hardly spoke on the rest of the trip. Thinking that she didn't much care for the silence, she turned on the radio to WABC, AM770, Cousin Brucie was on the air. It was very comforting to hear his voice after two months without any New York City-based radio station reception at Livingston Manor.

Through high school, he was the guy that we all listened to, playing the Top 40 hits; Motown, rock, whatever was popular with the teenagers. During the summers, if you were at the Jersey shore just hanging out on the beach, you would hear all the portable transistor radios blasting WABC, and likely Cousin Brucie. Walking down the beach on a crowded weekend you didn't need to take your radio because everyone was listening to Cousin Brucie and his playlist. You could walk a mile and not miss one song. But, that was then.

I spent the rest of the drive thinking about all that had happened over the last two months and how much things had changed for me. I tried to re-live every encounter with Annie; what she said, what I said and how we felt. If circumstances between us were different I'm sure that we'd soon be spending all of our time together. What if I was also going to be a high school sophomore, or we had both just graduated, or if we were enrolled at the same college; how convenient would that be?

What if I postponed my military service a few years? But the Army was never a contingency plan it was *the plan*. My decision to sign a commitment letter, a sort of pre-enlistment, was based on one precept alone; to accomplish something tangible, of real value to others, and myself too. Because Chris Bronson decisions are typically well thought out, they are not normally retractable, why would they be? I don't even know what trouble I would have in backing out of the Army deal. If I did back out, without a college deferment it is most highly likely that I would be drafted. Enlisting was always better than being drafted they say, able to choose between Army, Navy, Air Force or Marines with the possibility of some kind of support operation. If drafted, it pretty much meant the Marines, to Vietnam, to combat. Who really knew when the draft was going to end, if ever, but I didn't want the draft to be hanging over me, possibly for years, or as long as the war lasted.

I couldn't give a rat's ass what most people thought of me, but really, who would ever think that an Army private dating a high school sophomore was normal? I was able to avoid going to all of my own high school proms, now was not the time to start going to hers. From another angle, since I was turning eighteen in a couple of weeks, I took the time to look up the state statutes for sex with a minor. In law, it didn't seem to matter that she was going to be turning sixteen a couple of days after, still a minor. My concern and investigation was proof enough that I considered it inappropriate after I turned eighteen. Yes, it would be wrong "doing it" with an underage girl and yes, I considered all the consequences. And yet, I didn't want to think about it too much so that I could talk myself out of staying with Annie.

All of my friends were going off to college, you know, with Vietnam going on many were seeking a deferment. I think that I got wind of one other guy enlisting, everybody probably thought we were crazy, that's OK, let them think it. So, with all my friends away, it would be just Annie and I. That's fine too, but I know enough about her to understand that she likes to socialize with friends, that's what normal people have a tendency to do; so who are we going to hang out with? Her friends? I don't even know what sixteen year old girls like to do. With Annie, it's different, we have a lot in common, I don't know about any other sixteen year old.

But if, and that's a big if, I didn't fulfill my enlistment, and didn't go to college, what could I do in Ridgewood for the three years until Annie graduated? Sure, there were probably plenty of jobs at the mall in nearby Paramus but I didn't consider that alone much of an accomplishment, not for me, not for now. Then, what happens after three years, I hope that she would still want to go off to college, she's a smart girl and capable of almost anything, that's what I saw in her. Where would that leave me? College too? Again, I had to snap myself out of it, I needed to deal with reality, with the facts. Reality is such a bitch sometimes. I just couldn't see any of these scenarios working for us, so I decided to stick to my original plan, and if our relationship was real and permanent, nothing could stop it.

It was just after Labor Day when we arrived. Sally was glad to get home, I'm not so sure about me, the next two weeks weren't going to be easy. My mother and father were fine, invited my grandparents over to the house and prepared my favorite dinner in honor of my return; smoked kielbasa and pierogis, Polish on my mother's side of the family. They didn't believe half the stories that I told them about James Parrot, Max, Drew, Karl the baker, Stevie Ray catching on fire, Beth, Ruby and Miss Ahearn. I told them, "Really, nobody could have made this stuff up, it happened." They just laughed, we all did. I had gotten some letters from them while at Shandalee, maybe one a week and I always matched that with letters back, about me, what *I* was thinking and feeling, rather than details of other people they didn't even know.

Although I had written about the passing of Gabriel, I thought it would be better if I saved the sad details for when I saw them in person. Simply, it was quicker and less painful for me to write of his passing than call and get sucked into endless questions requiring details of his chilling murder. Of course they were in shock when I provided specifics of the events which put Bobby on a collision course with Gabriel and how it affected all of us at Shandalee, especially Miss Ahearn. My parents weren't happy that I didn't call them about that, but understood that there was nothing they could have done to help any of us. I sensed that they were projecting the specter of Gabriel's death to the perilous path ahead of me in the Army.

After dinner I took a break from the family and called Annie. Thank God she answered the phone so I didn't get an inquisition from one of her parents. Although I hadn't actually talked to her in the month since she left Shandalee, we had written each other every day. That's a lot of letters, but it seemed very normal to me, only because it was Annie. It was so good to hear the sound of her voice again and we seemed to pick up right where we left off in front of The Big House on her last day of camp.

"Chris, what are you doing tomorrow?" "Well, I hoped that we would get together later in the day, maybe six or seven, after dinner, maybe at the park." "I've got a better idea, let's drive down to the shore, it's really nice after Labor Day, all of the summer crowds are gone, I especially like Long Beach Island, it's more private there with lots of nice dunes by the water, you just have to know where to go. Heard on the radio that it's gonna be sunny all day." "Don't you have school?" "Yeah, but you'll be leaving soon and I want to spend as much time together as possible." "Me too Annie." "I'll cut classes, it won't even show that I'm absent if I get signed into homeroom. Anyway, this is still the first week of school and nothing's really going on. I just have to be back for work at *Petite's* at six, you can drop me off there, one of my parents will get me after work."

"I see that you've already given this a lot of thought, I don't like your cutting class, but we should just do it! I'll pick you up where?" "Woolworth's is good, I'll be at the lunch counter by nine, it's an easy walk from school." "I miss you so much Annie. This will be the first time that we'll be spending the whole day together, I can't wait." "Me too, see you tomorrow Chris, good night." "Good night sweetie."

Having hung up with Annie, I got back to the family and probably talked another hour before we had enough and turned in for the night. It was hard for me to fall asleep, too much was on my mind, about Annie of course and my leaving soon. I *wanted* to stay but I *needed* to go, that's who I am, still it was very sad for me, but I was intent to make the best of it for the time that we had left.

Then there was this little matter of not telling my parents about Annie. I weighed the pros and cons and determined that I would be running the risk of opening up a series of lectures or displeasure with the choices that I was continuing to make. This was nothing new, and for that reason I always avoided bringing girls around the house. I typically heard, "She didn't seem right for you," or "There are plenty of fish in the sea," in response to girls that just dumped me or, "I really liked her a lot," for girls that were ultimately exposed as mean or disingenuous. Why put myself through all that for someone that I am sure of? Maybe I was being a schmuck for not sharing my happiness with them, but I didn't want to complicate the situation any more than it already was. Who knows what time I finally fell asleep, it was two in the morning the last time I remember looking at the clock.

Full of anticipation I arrived early at Woolworth's and had a toasted *English Muffin* while I waited for Annie. Their lunch counter was nothing new to me. After school, about twice a week, some of my friends and I used to stop there as we walked home. My normal order would have been French fries and a vanilla Coke, too early for that today. You never knew which other classmates you would see at the Woolworth's counter. There was this one guy who seemed like a loner at school, maybe because he was passed over by most of the ruling cliques due to his obesity and funny hair. Maybe twice the weight of me, at least, I soon found him to be a rather jovial and interesting guy. At the counter he ruled, the cliques were left behind at school.

Then she appeared. I saw her as soon as she came through the front door, like I had radar able to detect her imminent proximity to me. I watched breathlessly as she walked down the wide aisles towards the lunch counter. As soon as I knew that she saw me I got up, she started running, and I prepared for her leaping into my arms, just like she did on her last day at Shandalee. I was not disappointed as she almost knocked me over again. We hugged and kissed and hugged and kissed, each not wanting to let the other go and not caring who was watching. As I let her back down to the ground I hoped that my brain was still working well enough to allow me to speak. "Annie, you look adorable. I can hardly believe this is really happening for us." How she moved and held herself left me spellbound. I think that I loved her hazel eyes more than anything else about her looks, they were kind eyes one rarely sees in a young person.

"You know Chris, I've been thinking about you every day, many times a day, all day since I came home. That's got to be hundreds of hours, and that doesn't even count the hours that I dreamt about you at night." "Stop, you're funny, but that's why I find you so irresistible. Do you want anything?" "No thanks, I ate at home." "Then we should go, let me pay up." "Did you pop a balloon so you know the price?" "Ha, that's only for banana splits, pop it and it could be you owe from one cent to thirty-nine cents. I tried a couple of times last year, think they're mostly thirty-something cents." The counter girl was clearly amused by all of our silliness so I left her a quarter tip, not bad since the *English Muffin* was only fifteen cents. The other morning patrons, mostly the same old men kibitzing over coffee or reading their newspapers were uninterested in our antics.

As we walked out her hand reached for mine and I accepted it willingly, I could not have been happier. "Oh wait, about face, I'm parked on Oak Street, let's go out the back through the pet department." "I should get you a baby turtle for your birthday Chris, they're so cute, they come with a little bowl and plastic palm tree. Look they only cost a dime and their little pond is only a quarter. I can afford it now, I'm working! Pick one out and I'll have them save it for you." "Yeah, I think I'll name it Annie, that sounds good! Let's go before I buy you a parakeet for *your* birthday, it's coming up too!" The whole thing was hilarious, maybe if we were five we would have begged our parents for turtles or parakeets for our birthday, but no longer.

"Annie, wait, stop, I do want to get you a gift, really. I've always wanted to do this but I never had anyone to do it for. I think I have a nickel, watch; I put the nickel in the machine, turn the dial to put my name in, C-H-R-I-S, and now yours, A-N-N-I-E, pull the handle and out comes the token. Here, read it!" "'Chris loves Annie,' I love it, can I keep it?" "Of course, I got it for you, an early birthday present," she laughed and put it in her pocket. "I really do like it, because it's from you."

"Here I am, hop in," as I unlocked the car for her. "And you say you bought this car for fifty bucks? It's nice, I saw it at camp, but we never had time to go for a drive, now we do," giving me one of those seductive looks. "You're so naughty Annie." "Just with you." She was getting me hot and she knew it. "Where's the seat belt Chris?" "Sorry, there are none, they only became law last year. Is your family's car new?" "Yes both of them." Unless I was going to ask what kind, it didn't seem like she was going to tell me. You wouldn't know it from the car that I drive, but since I was "car guy" I was curious. "What kinds?" "Mom drives the Pontiac GTO convertible and my stepfather, who is very conservative, drives his Fleetwood Brougham, a Cadillac you know. "Oh wow, that is so cool." "Yeah it is, but I don't like it when people think I'm some rich kid, that's not who I am. My father and step-father worked hard and we benefitted from that. I have to make my own way in life, together with you." She scooted over to me, maybe looking for reassurance for what she said, "Together with you." It was so easy to love Annie. I started the car, pulled her closer and put my arm around her for the rest of the trip.

She talked about West Virginia and the rest of her family, and I did too. It was like we were trying to catch up on years apart and today was a good day to accomplish all that. We had shared practically everything the first month at Shandalee. But, in spite of all my letters the second month, there were still a lot of details to fill in. "Hey, did you bring your bathing suit?" "Yes I did, I know you like my white bikini. It's in my bag, no math or history books today, just my suit, towels for us and some suntan lotion." "How about you?" "These cut-offs are my suit, makes it a lot easier. I'm so dark already, I don't even use suntan lotion at the end of the summer, what's the point?"

"Annie, I've been meaning to ask you but it never seemed like the right time." "Ask me about what Chris? You know that we share everything, you're my best friend." "Well, just before we made love in my room at Shandalee I asked you if we needed any protection and you said, 'not for me,' what did that mean?" "I don't want you to worry, but it is important that I explain, now's the right time. I got my first period when I was twelve but after a few months they stopped. My mother and I went to her gynecologist for an exam and she found that I had something called amenorrhea. It's not life threatening at all and has many remedies. I was told that if my periods didn't return normally after four months she would prescribe birth control pills to regulate my hormone production.

They didn't return so I started on the pill just as I was turning thirteen. I got my periods every month since, and when I eventually stop taking the pill, it is expected that I can get pregnant and have babies. Chris, you know that I want to have your babies someday." I wasn't shocked by any of this, I was so happy that she was treated, and many times I had thought about Annie and I having children. "I'm so glad that it worked out for you, it must have been a little scary. I have the same dream Annie, that we'll have children together." "Just so you know, you're the first boy that I ever slept with. Nobody except my parents and now you know I'm on the pill, God forbid if anybody at school found out, the boys are too horny as it is."

"I know where we can stop to pick up some lunch, it's an Italian deli in Belmar, they make the best subs. We can get some sodas and chips or whatever else you want. We're almost to Belmar, then another hour to the beach I think. We can eat once we get there." "Sounds good Chris." "That's it over there, I know it's not much of a place to look at. I'm going to get the same thing I always get, the Italian Special, if we get a whole one, we can split it, half is all I ever eat." "I want to have what you're having. Do you think they sell 'bug juice?'" "Ha, I wish they did, I loved that punch at camp!"

"Annie, you're going to have to direct me the rest of the way, I'm not so sure from here." "Of course, but first let's go down here," pointing the way. "I want to show you where I got my first surfboard." "I didn't know you were a surfer, that is so cool. Is it hard to do?" "Not anymore! There it is, *Ron Jon Surf Shop*, this is Ship Bottom, I like this beach too, but let's keep going. My father learned to surf with me when I was very young, that's the best time to learn. We both liked it no matter what the surf conditions, good or bad, it didn't much matter to us, just a lot of fun."

"I think just a few more minutes." "Annie this is so beautiful, no wonder you like to come here." "We've been here many times, but I like it best after Labor Day, no crowds. I'm looking for the turnoff, I think

it's pretty close so go slow. There it is, take the next left, down there."
"Wow, does anybody live down here?" "Not as of two weeks ago when
my family was here." "You picked the best spot ever, and I thought of
going to Seaside Heights, with the boardwalk and all that crazy stuff."
"You'll see. Park over there, on the road or we'll get stuck in the sand.
I think this is good." "Where can you change?"

"Right here silly, I'll get in the back, just watch out nobody
comes walking by." "OK, I won't look either." "Oh Chris, you've
already seen everything I've got, remember?" "You know I'll never
forget that day Annie, a bit risky but truly wonderful." She laughed as
she tried to undress, not so easy in the back seat of a compact Nova. It
simply doesn't make for a comfortable changing room. As she was
taking off her yellow sundress and panties I was compelled to turn
around. She had the face of an angel, smiling at me as she struggled to
get her bottom on, leaving her full bosoms exposed all the while. Before
attempting her top, she slowly reached up to grasp my hand resting on
the seat back and pressed it to her exposed breasts. She shut her eyes as
I gently caressed her. Then I closed mine to fix this intimate moment in
my mind forever.

"I brought a blanket for us, just bring your bag with the towels
and stuff. I'll get the ice cooler in the trunk, probably should have put
our lunch in it before, but we should be OK." It was only a fifty yard
walk through the sand to the beach, "Where do you want to sit Annie?"
"I don't know, maybe over there, by the dunes?" Leading the way she
found our perfect spot, our backs against the dunes and an unobstructed
ocean view. As promised, the beach was super nice; gone was the throng

of vacationers, lifeguards, chairs and multi-colored umbrellas polka-dotting the landscape, leaving only Annie and I, the welcoming sand dunes and the gently rolling surf of the ocean. An occasional seagull squawking about something, replacing the blasting of Cousin Brucie's Top 40. There wasn't anybody else to be seen up or down the beach, as far as I could see. Maybe understandable since Labor Day had passed and schools were back in session.

After leaving Woolworth's it was nearly a two hour drive to Long Beach Island, but it was worth every minute. Now almost noon and the sun straight above us at this time of year, things were beginning to heat up. "Let's jump in, I'm getting hot. Sorry I didn't have any air conditioning in the car, next car for sure." "Race you down Chris, first one in gets a free wish." I knew Annie was fast, but I guess she was faster than that, or maybe I liked the view from behind. "I won, I'll tell you my wish later," she exclaimed! The water was cold to me, even at this time of the year after the water temperature had steadily risen through the summer. Then again, once I got in past my waist and then my chest it was refreshing. We immediately embraced each other, kissed and started swirling our bodies around, holding on to each other and laughing the whole time. We couldn't keep our hands off each other, our desire to be one again was so powerful that even the chilly Atlantic water could not quench our passion.

"Let's dry off Chris, I'm having so much fun but we don't have all day, we should probably think about splitting by three-thirty." "That sounds about right, barring any major traffic delays you should be fine." We held hands as we walked up the gently sloping beach back to the blanket which I had spread. Now I was feeling like James Bond encountering the bikini girl. She reached into her bag and threw me one of the towels, and each of us dried off. "Really Annie, you give me the Minnie Mouse towel and you take the Road Runner one? It should be the other way around." "Oh, excuse me, who beat who to the water today? Don't worry, I won't tell anyone." I then watched as she bent over and grabbed one of the corners of the blanket and started dragging it into the dunes. As she looked over her shoulder back at me she let me know what her eyes already told me, "I'm going to collect on my wish now, coming?"

For the second time in an hour I was spreading our blanket in the sand, initially on which to have our lunch, now to prepare our bed. I helped her take off her top, and then bottom, then she to me. We made love for the rest of the afternoon, sometimes not knowing where her body ended and mine began, we were truly one again, like we were back at Shandalee. Annie was the kind of woman that I always wanted to be with but could never make the perfect connection to another mind and body, until now. Since she was the first girl that I was ever with, I hoped that my inexperience did not disappoint her.

We rarely stopped in between, only to profess our undying love and commitment to one another. The rest of the time consisted of rhythmic motions leading to crescendos of her calling out to God; "Oh God, oh God, oh God," over and over. Then murmured moans and finally full throated screams of pleasure as her whole body shook under mine. I was feeling the same sexual crescendos leading up to my own blasts from within. We both knew it was getting late but neither of us

119

wanted to be the first to say. Exhausted, our bodies were covered in sweat from the late summer sun, but to me she couldn't have been more beautiful. I adored Annie. So I did it, rolling off to her side I reluctantly announced, "Sweetheart, I think we missed lunch!" Catching her breath and laughing at the same time she noted, "I don't think either of us minded having dessert first." She tried to roll over onto me for more but slid off onto her back again.

"Chris, you know I can't go to work like this, what should we do?" "Well, we have the biggest bathtub right over there, the Atlantic Ocean, then we'll eat in the car on the way home, that's a start." We slowly put our suits back on and headed down to the water. No longer just holding hands as we walked, my arm draped over her shoulder and her arm around my waist, now seemingly inseparable. The water felt so good but we only stayed in a few minutes before drying off again. I ran over to the dune and retrieved our blanket, Annie got the other stuff and we headed back to the car. Although neither of us had a watch on the beach we guessed the time pretty good; quarter of four was the time on my car's reliable clock.

Annie went right to work pulling a brush through her hair, then air-drying it the best she could by opening the window once on the Parkway. We cooled off pretty quickly as we drove north at sixty. It's good that she had a cover-up and put it on as we pulled into the rest stop. I went into the building with her as she continued on to the ladies room to change back into her sundress. Reappearing shortly, she looked like we had never been to the beach or did what we did in the dunes, she was such a natural beauty. I never saw Annie wear any makeup, except for her subtle pink shade lipstick which didn't detract from her youthful allure. Once back on the road Annie opened the cooler and served lunch, still cold and delicious, talking about our subs.

Incapable of holding anything in, after a while she admitted, "I feel funny about not telling my parents about you, is that bad?" Thinking a bit, "I suppose that depends on why you chose not to tell them." "I don't know Chris, if you think it's about our age difference, it isn't. When you're eighty-five I'll be eighty-three, sounds the same to me," laughs and leans over to kiss my cheek. "I know what you mean, but always remember that I trust your judgement, whatever and whenever you decide." "Thanks, I feel better, but I don't like being sneaky."

"Chris, I saw something weird the other night. I had just got off work and it was obvious that something was going on at the park across the street. There were a bunch of police cars and cops standing by some wooden barricades, just watching. Inside the park, and you know how small it is, there were probably a hundred people protesting something, but I didn't know what at that point. As I stood there under the store awning I could hear there was someone with a bullhorn addressing the crowd. I didn't hear everything, but he was yelling about baby-killer soldiers, President Nixon and Vietnam."

"People are always protesting something in that park and I wouldn't have paid so much attention except for the steady rain that had begun about an hour before. It takes a lot to get anybody to stand out in the rain. What I mean is that they had to be really committed to whatever it was. Is that how people are beginning to think about the war? My parents would love you but they wouldn't understand why you would want to enlist to fight against the Vietnamese, especially my mother, a former campaign volunteer for Eugene McCarthy last year, that anti-war presidential candidate."

"Annie, I know what you're saying, but she has to understand that this is how I can best serve myself and my country right now. That will change, you've become a big part in planning my future. Best to keep us under wraps for now, neither of us needs any drama." Maybe feeling a little guilty for leaving Annie in a week I switched subjects again, "You know you got a little red from the sun today, good luck in explaining that when you get home!" The rest of the time we talked about how we would celebrate our birthdays coming up and what we wanted. We both knew that what we *wanted* was each other, but we already had that.

We made it back to *Petite's* with only ten minutes to spare. I asked her again if she wanted me to pick her up but she recommended that we stay with the original plan, one of her parents would get her. "Call me tonight?" "Of course Chris, I've got a phone in my room, so nobody will hear us." "Bye sweetie! This was the best day ever," she agreed. It was already after ten when she called and I hoped that the ringing hadn't woken up my parents, I grabbed the phone as fast as I could and got it on the first ring. I was so glad she called, the time didn't matter to me. The only thing that I had to do the next day was to be at the recruitment office in Hackensack at four, mainly to pick up my schedule for Basic Training and stuff. I still didn't know all the details. Even though she had school the next day we talked for two hours, mostly reliving the day's adventure.

The next day mom offered to drive me to the office but I declined, this was my thing and there was no reason to get her more upset than she was already. So I drove myself down and found it OK, a storefront in a small strip mall near the center of town. Nothing fancy from the outside, just a lot of enlistment posters in the window; a red, white and blue Uncle Sam proclaiming, *'I want you for US Army,'* along with all the others. What stood out among them was a poster picture of a teenage Negro under the banner, *'Your son can be Black and Navy too.'* Seriously, who would think that was an appropriate recruitment poster? I don't really know why, but I found it extremely offensive, maybe I was thinking of my friends James and Warren. Surely their parents wouldn't want this for those two, just as my parents didn't want this for me.

Once inside I was greeted by Captain Johnson who originally recruited me at the high school job fair, and spoke many times since. He gave me a lot of paperwork to take with me but quickly went over the most important parts. He had probably done this a hundred times before, probably within the last week alone. I learned that my new home for eight weeks was going to be Fort Campbell, Kentucky. After Basic Training I might stay there for eight more weeks of Advanced Infantry Training or be sent to another camp for the same thing, maybe Fort Dix, New Jersey. That, they'd tell me later. He explained that it may be easier for me to be dropped off at Fort Dix and take the Army bus to Kentucky, "You won't need your car down there," he added.

Then it struck me, all this time he's talking about *next* week, on my eighteenth birthday, on September tenth, just six days from now!

For a couple of minutes I must have zoned out while I was trying to figure how I'd tell Annie, and my parents too. I couldn't even think, this was going to be bad. Most of all, I was never so disappointed that I was going to miss a birthday, not mine, I didn't care a bit about that, but Annie's, two days later on the twelfth when she turned sixteen. It was Thursday today which meant that Annie was working the "long day" at *Petite's*, three-thirty to nine, so I wouldn't be able to tell her the bad news until she got home. But I couldn't wait, instead driving directly from Hackensack to Ridgewood, to *Petite's*.

"Hi Chris, what a surprise, here to shop for anybody's birthday?" "Maybe, you never know. What time is your break?" "Only my dinner break at six o'clock, can you wait twenty minutes? I have to help those customers, where can I meet you?" "Meet me in the park, take your time." "I want to hear all about your trip to Hackensack. Did it go well?" "I'll tell you all about it."

It was better that I leave the store and wait somewhere else, I didn't want to give the manager the impression that I was interfering with Annie's job. Work was important to me and for Annie too, it was in our nature. I probably hadn't been in the park for two years, only going in to cut across to the small bus stop adjacent to it. To pass the time while waiting for Annie I read each of the small memorial plaques honoring the American servicemen and women from Ridgewood who died in action. The modest gray granite pedestals, placed on the four corners of the park, displayed the cast bronze plaques with each of their names from the Civil War, World War I, World War II and the Korean War. Now that the four corners were taken, I wondered where the monument honoring the dead from the Vietnam War would be placed? Or would there be any acknowledgement?

I don't know for sure but, based on traces of red paint still on the bronze plaques, it looked like someone had recently cleaned up graffiti or vandalism, perhaps left over from the "protest" that Annie had told me about. Since I had arrived back in Ridgewood and started reading newspapers again I was beginning to see that the antiwar movement was real and growing. Still, it was disheartening to me that the names of those who gave their lives so that we could live free would be desecrated in such a cowardly manner. But, what did I expect? You couldn't escape the depravity taking place in America.

Daily, never skipping a day, I was either reading or hearing about some of the most shameful perversions; wealthy families and movie stars being executed in their Los Angeles homes, and US Senator Ted Kennedy drunk driving a young intern into a river, leaving her to drown in six feet of water. New York City police clashing with some homosexuals at one of their local bars. The Black Panther Party, Students for a Democratic Society, Youth International Party, Yippies you know, and the Weather Underground were confusing to people like me, what did they want? A countercultural revolution? At no time did I ever think that they represented me, *I represented me.* Through all their righteous words I saw hate and an underlying desire to destroy America. And more than anybody else, I wanted to see the end to the Vietnam War and an end to the protests.

I was overthinking everything today so I rested on a bench under a most unusual tree. Looking around I saw another plaque, this one just painted wood staked into the ground, simply identifying it as a "Gingko Tree." It was a different kind of tree, oriental in appearance and not much of a shade tree. Very tall and narrow with fan-shaped leaves, not anything like the broad umbrella of shade provided by the maple trees elsewhere in the park. It was there that I waited for Annie, under the gingko tree.

"Boo!" "Oh my gosh, you scared me Annie." "Sorry, I just couldn't resist sneaking around the back. Where do you want to go for dinner? How 'bout the Daily Treat, I like their sandwiches." "OK, but before we go, sit with me, I want to tell you about Hackensack." "Sure Chris, how did it go?" "So, I met with the recruiter and he gave me bunches of stuff to read but when we were talking about leaving for boot camp he's saying September tenth." "On your birthday? That's crazy, how can you get ready so soon." "I'm ready now, the point is that I didn't want to leave next week, I was expecting to stay for your birthday." "I'm sorry Chris, I was looking forward to spending it with you too." As tears began to well up in her eyes I could see that reality was beginning to set in for Annie, I reached for her hand and squeezed it tightly, but that wasn't enough to stem the flow of tears to come. I just didn't know what to say, neither did she, so we just sat on the bench, embracing each other like it would be the last.

Maybe we were just too young to know how to deal with our new love, or maybe it was just me, too stubborn or selfish to change my plans for her, or anybody else. It seems that I had unintentionally painted the two of us into a corner, where there were no longer any options. She wanted me and I wanted her, my gosh, she even told me that she wanted to have my babies, it was so simple, now seemingly impossible. "C'mon Annie, please stop crying, let's go for a walk." Through the tears, "Alright Chris." "You've gotta get back soon, I'll buy you dinner at Woolworth's, it's closer."

Hand in hand, we walked up two blocks and crossed over to Woolworth's. By that time, Annie had calmed down a bit. Unlike Annie, who showed her emotions and expressed herself readily to me and probably everyone else, I was agonizing over our looming separation and feeling a deep pain, unable to drive it out. Now trying to put on a happy face, "Hey, they have a lot of balloons up on the wall Chris, feel like a banana split?" "Yeah, you and James, you're in good company." "What do you mean?" "James could eat a banana split for lunch, dinner too probably." We sat at the counter like we did when we met for our shore trip. Both of us avoided talking about next week, I couldn't bear to see Annie cry again.

"I don't want you paying for my dinner, this is a work dinner, so let's pop our own balloons and pay whatever they say." "Really Annie, I feel so bad but if you want a little friendly competition I'm up for it. Miss, we're done now can we check out, first the balloons. Give each of us one, she thinks she's gonna win tonight. Annie, you pop first." "No, let's see yours first." So, I stuck a fork into my balloon, revealing the amount written on a tiny slip of paper. "Oh no, thirty-nine cents, the best I can hope for is a tie!" "Your turn, just jab it?" She popped hers like a pro. "One cent! "Are you kidding me?" "Guess I'm just lucky Chris, do you have change of a nickel?" "Not funny Annie," both of us laughing now.

We walked back to *Petite's*, kissed goodnight and promised to talk tomorrow. My next order of business was to deliver the details of my departure to my parents. I wasn't sure which was going to be worse, the reaction I already got from Annie or that of my parents. It went terribly, mom cried and after a while dad ushered her off to their bedroom for the rest of the night. I went to my room, ate some pistachio nuts and then fell asleep lying on top of my bedspread in my street clothes. At some point I must have undressed and climbed under the covers, don't even remember doing it.

The goodnight kiss in front of *Petite's* would be the last time that I would see Annie before leaving for boot camp. I had really screwed everything up. I called the next day after school let out but her mother picked up the phone saying that she was at "play practice." I just told her that I was, "Chris from school," and gave her my number for Annie to call me back. Annie had already told me that she had signed up for the high school play production of *The Music Man*. I was very proud of her landing a leading role, of librarian Marian Paroo, very cool. Between *Petite's*, play rehearsal and my having to visit relatives before I left we played phone tag for a week, then I was gone. It was a long bus ride to Fort Campbell, thinking about everything that I had just given up made the trip so much longer. I didn't really know how she still felt about me. I didn't even like me!

 Chapter XI

# The Screaming Eagles

Basic Training was not as terrible as some people had warned, but most of them had never even been through it, so they wouldn't have known squat anyway. Although I didn't have any real form of physical exercise the whole summer I was still in pretty good shape from high school basketball the last two years, just JV. Every day at Basic was the same as the day before; up at five, running, breakfast, skills training at the firing range or hand-to-hand combat, then lunch, then more running and instruction. I was issued a M16 rifle and 38 caliber pistol, I learned them well, I had to, my life could depend on it.

I met this guy Peter at Basic, also from Jersey, we were in the same platoon and became fast friends. He may not have been the fastest man in the platoon, but without question the strongest, a rock of a man. I even told him, "You might not be the quickest, but the only man capable of carrying any one of us out on his back." His name was Peter but mostly we called him Pastor since he would frequently be praying, out loud for everyone to hear. He wasn't crazy, actually the exact opposite, he reminded me of James, my mentor from Shandalee. It was always good to have Pastor around, a great guy, trusted friend and would turn out to be a good soldier. Funny thing, I never heard him praying for himself, always for the rest of us.

Basic Training ended on a Friday and I was required to continue at Fort Campbell for Advanced Infantry Training, which meant that I was being assigned to the Army's 101st Airborne Division, better known as the "Screaming Eagles." I was designated 3rd Brigade, 2nd Battalion Infantry and Pastor to artillery, same fort, different programs, but we still hung out when we were off. Understandably, the Army doesn't let *you* pick a training program, *it* picks. Could have been in something else too, like the motor pool, which would have been OK. The Screaming Eagles had a long and decorated history in the Army. I read that they were crucial in World War II, especially during the D-Day landing and airborne operations in Normandy, France.

Back in Ridgewood, when I was making my decision to enlist, one of the naysayers told me to avoid being drafted because, "You could wind up in the infantry or worse yet, in the Screaming Eagles where you would surely be sent to Vietnam." I knew that he was looking out for me, what he thought was in my best interest, but now how ironic, I enlisted and still likely to follow the same path to Vietnam. Whatever the path, I was now a proud Screaming Eagle! Somehow I felt much different than the screaming eagles beloved by James at Shandalee, "Striking down from the skies," I remembered him saying. Soon we were sent to Vietnam.

Everyone was talking about the monsoon season in the highlands, further north than where I was initially stationed in Nam. Some said the rains began in September, others said beginning in November. No matter when, it could produce twenty inches of rainfall a day. I asked, "Per day? Not per week or month?" Per day seemed to be the consensus. That meant that I was going to be staying put in the flatlands for a few months, at least until the weather cleared enough to make mountain combat possible again. Still, moving north to the higher elevations meant closer to the greatest concentration of VC and likely an increase in firefights, I hoped that I was prepared.

In early March my unit commander received orders that we would be relocating north to rebuild an abandoned firebase, Firebase Ripcord, a hilltop in the mountains north of Da Nang, overlooking the A Shau Valley. The exact history of this firebase wasn't really clear to me but we heard that the hill had been American-occupied a year or two ago, for the same objective that we now being given. We would be responsible for re-establishing our cannon firepower on a hilltop, one that we had previously held. The main purpose of this firebase is to blast away, disrupt and destroy any war material supply logistics coming from North Vietnam to supply the PAVN and VC. To us, the People's Army of Vietnam and the Viet Cong were all the same so we lumped everyone in together; their armed allies, regulars, militia and anybody who wanted to kill us we just called VC, easier that way. The Ho Chi Minh Trail was such a transportation route extending from North Vietnam down into Laos and Cambodia.

Early in March of 1970, about six months after I reported to Basic Training, I was promoted to Staff Sergeant, one level above a Sergeant and one below Sergeant First Class. I don't know what exactly the Army saw in me but some things you just shouldn't question. It wasn't made clear if I was going to be placed in charge of a squad, which could be announced later I thought. One of the other guys, who waited the customary six *years* before the same promotion, told me not to get too excited, the Army had lost a lot of sergeants in Vietnam and were now promoting as fast as they could. In charge, or not in charge, I was here to do a soldier's duty and go home, the rest had little meaning to me.

I was on the first wave of helicopters designated to land at the firebase, maybe forty Bell UH-1D aircraft, we just called them "Huey's." I was riding with nine infantrymen, the squad they warily put me in charge of, and a bunch of supplies. Twelve troops and a crew of two was the normal limit for the Huey, and the best that I could figure, was possibly six stretchers to evacuate any wounded if necessary. Twelve going in and maybe six dead or wounded going out, not so easy to wrap my mind around. These same Huey's and pilots were our only lifeline in and out and would supply us with all the necessities; munitions, food and medical supplies. Today we flew with the doors pinned back so we had a good view of our new home as we got closer.

It was rugged and inhospitable, there was no way to sugarcoat this mess. It looked like somebody or something had whacked off the top of this hill in a wrathful final judgement. It was barren, no trees, no vegetation, no nothing. Plant life had simply given up here, every other plant or animal survivors already washed away by the unforgiving monsoons. The dirt and dust was now beginning to swirl outward from our approaching Huey. There were abandoned foxholes and craters in every direction, making landing more challenging for the pilots. As our helicopter prepared to land I heard the first enemy mortar shell explode, the second one I saw off to our right.

The next few months went by slowly, living conditions were crowded, leaving personal space a luxury, if you could find it. I stopped writing Annie, she was so sweet that it had become painful to be writing from such an ugly place. I had become spiritually lost, no longer knowing what to pray for. I was now believing that it came down to two

133

options; either pray to kill every one of the enemy or, if I were to die, it would be quick and painless. How could they be my only choices? Every day I feel like I am playing a depraved game of "King of the Mountain." The kids' game where you try to get to the highest point of a hill, then struggle to push the others off. You could never win because as you shoved one down another would reach the top to do the same to you, and over and over again until all participants become exhausted from an unwinnable game. Complicating matters, there were only a few hundred of us left at Firebase Ripcord and probably a few thousand VC, making it impossible for us to sustain King of the Mountain here.

My fire team squad was typically on patrol just south of Firebase, sometimes for three or four days, not long by Army standards, but no stand down, unless you actually considered returning to Ripcord "downtime." When operating in the field we would regularly come across the VC and engage in small firefights. Mostly we killed or expelled them from the area.

To the north of Ripcord we would send forward observers beyond the perimeter, sometimes as far as five miles. If the enemy was spotted, the position was called in and we would shell the hell out of them with the Howitzer's from our two artillery batteries, capable of hitting anything within a fifteen mile radius.

Unlike the flatlands far south of us, any activity we saw north of Firebase was enemy related. There were no civilians up in the mountains "just going about their business." It didn't lead to any confusion about who the enemy was, we just killed them all. The Ho Chi Minh supply trail was always active, not continuously, but intermittently by trucks, ox carts, bicycles and once we even saw elephants loaded with bundles on their backs, probably food or ammo supply, or both. It was surreal, not a dream since we all saw it. So, we swung the big cannons around and blew the gray beasts up, all of them.

But, toward the end of June as the frequency of enemy mortar attacks increased, I didn't think it was any safer being on Firebase than anywhere on patrol. We were vulnerable either way. The VC were all over, we could see them at any time of day. As we were watching them, they were measuring us up for later. Firebase was suffering heavy casualties as the VC had been gaining control of the four surrounding hilltops, each within a couple of miles and capable of hitting us with mortars. I was on watch duty early morning July 1$^{st}$ and was about to change out when I was hit by shrapnel from one of them. At first I didn't even know that I was hurt but after reaching back to my left thigh, I confirmed the "wet" that I felt was my own blood. Then the burning started, I called for help as I sat.

I didn't have to wait long to be airlifted to the Naval Support Activity Station Hospital in Da Nang. Like I had imagined on the Huey ride which first brought me to Firebase Ripcord, I was now one of six lying on canvas stretchers jostling around on the helicopter floor. As we became airborne I'm still hearing small arms enemy fire whizzing by. For the enemy who had wished us dead, was it not enough for them that we might already be half dead? At what point would their thirst for blood be quenched? As the morphine drip from the bottle hanging from the hook over my head erased all my bodily pain I reached out and held the hand of the soldier lying next to me, thinking it was Annie. I didn't understand until later that the soldier had been killed at Firestop, as well as the four others, I was the only casualty, the rest were already dead before they were loaded into the Huey.

I don't remember much more from the short trip to Da Nang but I do remember asking the medic on board, "Do you think I'm going to be sent home?" "You'll be fine, nobody's ever sent home from Da Nang, the road home for them is through Okinawa, you know, Japan. These others will be transferred there today. Look, it's not the best way to make it home because you will either be dead already, die there from the catastrophic injury which sent you there, or so beyond repair that you can't be sent back into battle. Me, I'm hoping to finish out my tour and go home in one piece."

Not exactly what I was asking but I understood his meaning. I was grateful that it was only a minor wound. The doctors were quick to remove a metal fragment, stitch me up and give me some needed rest time. I was sent back to Firebase in four days. Even as I was returning through an increased level of mortar and rifle fire I was glad to be back, to finish what I had started out to do. Pastor had heard of my return and was the first to greet me.

Each day in the next few weeks saw a greater increase in enemy activity and Firebase casualties. I was growing concerned. In an effort to determine the intensity of the increased VC activity toward Firebase, my platoon set out north where the greatest buildup seemed to be coming from. Were we seeing a burst or was this the beginning of an all-out siege to destroy us? On the morning of July 22nd we were relatively undetected by the enemy so we pushed out nearly five miles the first day. But, just before dusk, we were under constant attack by small pockets of the enemy. They were mostly killed, taking them out with the M-79 grenade launchers which Pastor and others carried. Fortunately, there wasn't any hand-to-hand combat the first day, that would soon change.

In the morning of the second day the level of VC resistance was basically the same, just pockets, so we continued to push father out. In contact with Firebase since we left, they were now telling us that the enemy mortar attacks had escalated significantly and Firebase Ripcord had become indefensible. The orders were to return immediately! We would soon discover that since starting out, the VC had positioned themselves between us and Firebase, forcing us to go *through* them if we wanted to rejoin our Battalion. So we set out to do just that. Our platoon leader, Sergeant First Class Robbie Dempko, was out front when the next enemy mortar hit. He was a nice man, an elementary school teacher who was very proud of his continuous service in the Army Reserve, what he called his "part time job." He died instantly, two others closest to him weren't so lucky, they hung on for five minutes then closed their eyes for the last time.

We tried to find cover as we exchanged rifle fire but we were being cut down mercilessly. Our grenade launcher was effective in inflicting some damage but ultimately we could neither defend our position nor push through the VC. The VC were well dug in and our platoon firepower would not be sufficient to cause the VC to retreat around us.

Short on options, I gathered up all the smoke grenades available, then signaled the squad to spread out. I tried to inform the other squad leaders of our last ditch effort to push through, but they were either dead, dying or wounded. Without a platoon leader to stop me, we threw all that we had directly in front of us, first the grenades and then our M16's. We all ran like hell, straight ahead, directly to the enemy. Once seeing our plan, the other squads immediately followed.

We quickly encountered the VC and had to engage in hand-to-hand combat. It was unimaginable, former combatants now lay dying side-by-side. We lost a lot of men within the first thirty minutes but only gained a hundred yards before we had to dig in again and try to hold our new position. As a new barrage of mortar shells started raining down, a new wave of VC had amassed to our rear, ensuring our certain death. Unwilling to give in or risk surrender to a maddened VC, I radioed Firebase, told the commanding officer of our desperation and suggested that unless he starting blasting away with the Howitzer's we would all die within the hour. He asked to speak to the platoon leader, but just silence after I told him that he had been killed. "What's your name soldier?" "Staff Sergeant Christopher Bronson, sir." Then silence again, squandering still more of the precious little time left before being overwhelmed by the VC, "what are your coordinates?" "Who the hell knows, we're five miles out, directly north, blast away for ten minutes then cease fire, that's all the time we need."

I felt that I had not effectively conveyed our dire situation. I was now begging, "Please do what I ask, I know it's crazy, but it's our only hope to get the VC to retreat to clear our path. I know that I may die in the process, but many of us may have a chance to make it back. "Please, I am begging you." I don't know what ran through his mind but to me, this was our only hope to escape this hell, our only way out.

Through the cacophony of battle sounds I heard Pastor's voice above all others, not engaged in fighting any longer, not lying low to the ground like all of the rest of us, but kneeling in prayer. He had taught me this prayer at boot camp and although it might have seemed like madness to others at this moment, I understood better than I ever had. His was not a quiet prayer today, he was yelling for everyone to hear, enemy alike, at the top of his lungs, as if he was challenging any living thing to try to break God's hedge of protection that he was so earnestly seeking. He called out;

*"The Lord is my shepherd; I shall not want.*
*He maketh me to lie down in green pastures.*
*He leadeth me beside the still waters.*
*He restoreth my soul: He leadeth me in the paths of*
*righteousness for his name's sake.*
*Yea, though I walk through the valley of the shadow of death,*
*I will fear no evil: for thou art with me.*
*Thy rod and thy staff they comfort me.*
*Thou preparest a table before me in the presence of mine enemies.*
*Thou anointest my head with oil; my cup runneth over.*
*Surely goodness and mercy shall follow me all the days of my life.*
*And I will dwell in the house of the Lord forever."*

Upon his finishing, like on cue, the 155MM Howitzer shells began to burst all around us. Jubilant, I jumped up and began to run home screaming, "Thank you God, thank you God, thank you, save us all." The bombardment seemed to totally confuse the VC as they ran in the opposite direction. It was confounding, they were running in one direction and we in the other, sometimes right past each other, neither of us firing our weapons any longer. As we sprinted towards Firebase we were discarding most of our equipment, anything that slowed us down was no longer of any value. The Firebase cannons continued to pound away, shells falling randomly among us and the fleeing VC; we ran straight.

Just as the shelling seemed to slow, I turned around to see if my old friend Pastor was still OK. I was relieved when I spotted him just a couple yards back. "We're gonna make it, we're gonna make it, we're going home, keep running," I shouted out. With my last word the force of the next blast threw me to the ground in a blinding flash of light, leaving me face down in the dirt. Everything fell silent for me but I felt a strong force lift me from the ground and carry me along, I felt no pain. It must be Pastor, thank God for Pastor. "Annie! Annie-e-e-e-e! I'm going home."

# Chapter XII
# **Going Home**

Da Nang triage was more bustling than my last visit, more doctors, more nurses, all scurrying around in an effort to save us. It was confusing for me, I couldn't speak, hear, nor feel anything. Yet, my eyes were wide open to see the hundreds coming and going in the chaos. I just put my trust in God. I knew that many of those with me in battle today did not make it to Da Nang, we had to leave their lifeless bodies behind as we fought and clawed our way back to Firebase. I would never know how many of us made it back. I wasn't being told anything.

I hoped and prayed that someone at Da Nang would make a determination that I was worth saving. After a month it seemed like my condition still hadn't changed. During the day and sometimes at night I just stared up at the ceiling. The nurses would look me over every few hours and I welcomed their visits. I had no idea what they thought was wrong with me. From what I was able to see they went about their business very quickly and rarely spoke. There was no time for chatter as they were all so busy administering to the others as quickly as they could. Nobody in my section was being fed solid foods so I figured that I was being kept alive through an IV. At no time did I lose hope for a full recovery, I had to remain positive, I had to get home, there were people waiting for me! She was waiting for me!

Sometimes I felt that all that was left of me was my head, no hands, no feet, and no body. By the time they ordered my transfer to the US hospital in Okinawa I was cleaned up quite well, in appearance only. If somebody had put me in scrubs and propped me up at a desk, everyone would think that I was a young doctor. No visible wounds or scars on me, eyes wide open, getting ready to make the rounds to see my patients. Long gone were the blood-soaked field bandages which once bound me together as I arrived at Da Nang the first time.

I was being transferred to the hospital in Okinawa, a very long plane ride I thought. Everything was much more secure during the flight, certainly nobody still shooting at us, no clanging IV bottle and no rolling around on the floor. Instead, I was comfortably strapped into a gurney, not the canvas stretcher that carried me to the evac helicopter a month ago. It did seem strange to me that I was the only patient on the plane. Was I the only survivor from the July 23rd firefight or was I getting special treatment because I was one of the Screaming Eagles? Neither made sense.

Okinawa was as good a hospital as any I had seen back home. I had been to the hospital three times when I was a kid, all broken arms, three different times, wrist, forearm and then elbow. I was very active and liked to play sports but I was also very skinny and became clumsier as I went through several growth spurts. Since I joined the Army I had grown three inches and gained some twenty pounds. Yet throughout, I remained in the upper tenth percentile in Army's physical assessment, probably no longer, I couldn't even stand up.

The chaos that I saw in Da Nang was not present here. It was no longer triage, more like specialized long term care for the dying and wounded. Everything was clean, bright and orderly, those providing for my care were all dressed in white, absent were any blood stains from their shifts in the OR. I now spent most of my time in a deep sleep, perhaps all that I needed to regain my strength to return home. My room was no longer shared with other soldiers, I was by myself day and night, except for an occasional attendant. I even thought that I saw my other grandfather once, but he had died years ago, I must have been drugged up still. It was odd to me that they never turned the lights off, wouldn't it help people trying to get to sleep?

Being sidelined so long, I had all the time in the world to think about things. I shouldn't say "things," but rather people, the same ones I loved or who loved me. Even the ones with whom I had disagreements or treated me unfairly gave me reason for further consideration. I was beginning to see that I was often mistaken in my judgement, of people I mean. My first impression of some people was simply wrong, as I had misjudged Beth and Gabriel. Same thing with Bobby, but in his case, believing early on that he was a cool dude, which he wasn't. By my own hand, through nobody else, I failed to protect my own best interest, or even that which could have resulted in a greater good. In the case of Annie, I knew from the first meeting, but then chose to minimize and ultimately disregard the greater good for Annie and I. I should never have left, and for that I was truly sorry, I needed to tell her.

Still, I knew nothing about my transfer back to the states. I felt that I was ready but day after day there was no news. I completely lost track of time, not knowing if I was in Okinawa for months, or even years. There was simply no longer any way for me to measure time. Then, one day, who knows what day it was, one of the doctors arrived with several attendants to move me to another room, so I believed. I knew him from Da Nang, a nice man with a kind look about him, Dr. Sommer was his name. I felt like I was in good hands. As they moved me out we just kept going and going until I boarded what I think was an

AirMed plane. It was wonderful, more attendants than I had already seen anywhere. I was happy to see that Dr. Sommer was going to be making the trip with me. Where else could we be going except home? I was euphoric, crazy happy.

I must have fallen asleep for the long trip but I could see that we were back on American soil, in Ridgewood, New Jersey, in Valley Hospital where I was born and where they repaired my broken bones years before. My new room was perfect; fresh and clean and bright, even better than the one in Okinawa. No longer a single room, I now shared it with another man, a vet, just like me. I already thought of myself as a vet, someone who *had* served their country, but was no longer in the armed services, or not in combat for sure. I couldn't understand why, but at all times they kept my roommate and I separated by one of those privacy curtains. Something else quite peculiar since my arrival at Valley Hospital was that my hearing had returned and my speech was restored.

Time passed quickly as I became friends with my roommate and spent most of our waking hours talking. Mostly it was me talking about my family, Shandalee and especially Annie. He was a very good listener, it's what I needed after my injury had silenced me for such a long time. On some days he probably thought I'd never shut up about her. I never spoke about Nam, Firebase Ripcord or the Screaming Eagles, they were no longer my responsibility, priority or duty. Soon I was up and sitting in the lounge chair next to the window. I enjoyed gazing out as people were coming and going through the hospital doors. I always wondered who they were, some people looked sad, others looked happy, sometimes the difference between a terminal illness and the birth of a new baby in the family, or somewhere in between, I would never really know. Through my window I'd see hospital staff use their lunch breaks to take walks on nice days; onto the sidewalk of North Van Dien Avenue, turning left onto Linwood Avenue, through the rear parking lot, around the hospital and back onto North Van Dien before coming in or taking another lap.

It was probably one of the ten best days of the year, a cloudless mid-summer day, just lying in bed thinking about practically everything important to me when I saw her walk in. She was as beautiful as ever, it was my Annie. She carried a bouquet of flowers which quickly filled the room with the sweet aroma of lily-of-the-valley. "Annie, is it really you, I've missed you so much, I have a lot to tell you. Thank you for the flowers, they remind me of The Playhouse. Did you know the lily-of-the-valley represents happiness, devotion and restoration of one's soul? Sorry, I'm jibber-jabbering, I'll stop. Here, sit, tell me everything I missed since I left." She came over, set the flowers on the bed next to me, knelt and laid her head down with mine and closed her eyes.

I saw Dr. Sommer the next morning and he informed me that I was well enough to leave the hospital, but only for the day, "Nothing strenuous I warn you, and you must be back by six o'clock." I was incredibly happy to hear the good news, "Thank you Dr. Sommer, thank you so much, I don't even know what to do first." "You'll figure it out Chris, make it count, let's see how you do."

Annie came to get me the very next morning. First I had to sign some kind of Hospital Release Pass before they came with a wheelchair to deliver me to the pickup-drop-off area. I really don't know why they do the chair thing, I felt fine, I felt great! Annie had gone ahead of us to get her car and was already at the pickup as we arrived. "Oh my, you got your mother's GTO, this is fantastic." As she drove I talked and talked, there was so much to explain and apologize for. She knew what I was talking about. "How does one person fall in love, then run away for some indefensible reason, then stop writing, leaving them alone? I'm so sorry Annie and ask that you forgive me." We drove for a couple of hours, I didn't even ask where we were going, it didn't matter.

Boy, was I surprised when we pulled up in front of Tony's Tavern in Livingston Manor. "Oh Annie, you always know what I like, you're the best." It only got better, when we walked in, some people at one of the tables in the back started yelling and waving to us. It was the old gang from Shandalee; Max, Drew, John, and my dear friend James. It warmed my heart to see the love they still had for one another. As we approached closer they yelled out to Annie. I was so choked up I couldn't even speak, they must have known that I had been to Nam and was coming back to visit today. Annie, also tearing up said, "Thank you Kitchen Boys, it means a lot." After, it was non-stop stories of that fabled 1969 summer in the Catskills.

It was so sad to hear that Beth had passed away a year ago, some kind of cancer someone said. I was still ashamed of how I misread her, one of the camp's best! Nobody had heard anything about Bobby since he was convicted and went to prison, probably still a lost soul, but always worthy of our prayers.

Drew said he's at Ohio State University and was a member of the Sigma Phi Epsilon social fraternity. He was even wearing a Sig Ep tee shirt. I always knew that if he could gain the trust, confidence and acceptance of The Kitchen Boys, anything was possible for him.

"Listen everybody," Drew now standing, "Something big I've got to tell you. My aunt, you know, Miss Ahearn, moved in with us, to Ohio, so a year later she meets someone! Ready, she's going to be moving out in the fall when she gets married! She's so happy, I never thought I'd see the day!" I was also very excited for her, if anybody, she deserved it.

Always the understated one who never liked to talk about himself, Max made his mark at Woodstock and is a record producer in New York City. We all knew it would happen sooner or later. "Follow your dream," was the only advice that he was willing to offer the rest of us.

"Just like Warren," James added. "He always talked to me about becoming a chef. I knew he wasn't talking about a chef like *our* Chef in the camp kitchen who thought that he was the only one capable of making the bug juice every day. It was the simplest thing; add five cups of the fruit-flavored powder to five gallons of water, how could anybody screw that up? Chef would never admit that Warren's skills were far superior to his in the kitchen. Warren called me last night to say sorry that he couldn't be here for our little reunion. He's enrolled at the Culinary Institute of America, actually near here, but has weekend classes. However, he confessed that he still sees Kirsten from time to time, imagine that! They always did make a cute couple."

"But not as cute as Annie and Chris," as he raised his glass to Annie seated next to him and began to sing, then the rest joined in;

> *"Here's to Brother Chris, he's a friend of mine,*
> *drink to him from your glass of wine.*
> *Brother Chris is the one we cheer,*
> *drink to him from your mug of beer.*
> *Keep him close 'cause he's your friend too,*
> *a nicer guy we never knew."*

As Annie started to tear up again, James wanted to change the subject quickly, "John what have you been up to?" "You're funny James, you tell them!" "Nope, it's your turn Brother." "Well, I'm in the Seminary at Princeton University, I know, don't laugh too hard, that's my true calling and it's what I want for my life's work. So, I'm at the coffee shop on campus and guess who comes swaggering in?" "I don't swagger, do I?" "Let me finish telling the story James. In *walks* James. He'll never tell you, but Princeton gave him a four-year, full-boat academic scholarship. Funny, I never really thought he was too bright!" Everyone laughed and then booed John, all in good fun.

I can't believe that Annie has already graduated from high school and will be going to Rutgers in the fall, as pre-med. She always knew what she wanted and made everything look so easy as she spread joy wherever she went. I wish that I had paid more attention and learned that lesson from her.

I think that everyone, that is everyone except me, knew that Camp Shandalee was closed down after the summer of 1969. But, because of his Aunt, Drew had some more inside information. "The gossip, hearsay and truth about Gabriel's murder was too much for the United Christian Women's Association to bear. A developer bought the property and built a bunch of vacation homes there. That's a shame, I loved that summer and I love all of you, especially Chris who taught me so much." OK Drew, we love you too, my little buddy.

After a couple of hours it was time to go home, a lot of hugging followed in between the familiar promises to "keep in touch." I was feeling tired, closed my eyes and fell asleep for most of the ride back to the hospital.

It wasn't long before Dr. Sommer arrived in my room. "Did you have a nice day Chris?" "I surely did, it was the best day ever." "So you got to visit with Annie, Max, Drew, John and James all day, but did you tell them everything that you wished you had said before?" "Yes, it was great." "Good, that's what I wanted to hear." As he now stood between my bed and that of my roommate he swung his arm to push back the curtain which had been separating us since I arrived. "Chris, Peter, it's time for us to go." "What? Pastor, what are you doing here? I didn't know it was you, your voice, you sound different." "I know, on our side we all sound 'different.' Don't freak out. I had to come with you from Nam."

"I don't understand what's happening, Dr. Sommer help me understand." "Brace yourself Chris. You and Peter never made it back to Firebase Ripcord, you were both killed instantly from the same blast.

It was I who lifted you both up to carry you away. I couldn't let either of you suffer any longer for the Bible says that, 'Greater love hath no man than this, that a man lay down his life for his friends.' Although your life was lost, your last order enabled the rest of your platoon to reach Firebase safely." "And why Pastor?" "He was following right behind you, also knowing the risk. As your platoon continued to push forward and scramble in, Firebase was being evacuated. After your last man boarded the Huey, your B-52 bombers lay waste to the entire zone. Wave after wave they came, carpet bombing until the jungle was laid bare of every living thing."

Pastor spoke again, "When we fell in that jungle I was ready to go home to my Father, but my Guardian believed that I needed to remain with you, until you found absolution, no matter how long it took. Our Guardian can explain better." "Yes, I'll try to explain. You know me as Dr. Sommer, I'm Hans Sommer, who Peter calls your 'Guardian.' Just call me Hans as I am no longer a doctor and have not been for years."

"When you fell you were not yet ready to be with the Father, not until you could rid yourself of all guilt and relieve yourself of any earthly duty which may still have bound you, no matter how long it took." "But, how long have you been waiting for me?" "We have been here with you to watch three winters come and go, three earthly years." "Is my name and face familiar to you Chris, before Da Nang?" "No, not at all." "Maybe if I use my earthly voice, the one with a distinct Austrian accent you will remember me." "How can it be? Annie's father?"

"Yes, I have been with you since you first sat with Annie on the porch at Shandalee, walked in the woods to the serpent, you saw me there, at Woolworth's lunch counter twice, how do you think she got the sundae for a penny? I was even in the dunes with you at Long Beach Island, but we'll talk about that later." "Oops, sorry about that Hans, I loved her that much." "And she truly loved you." "Go back a minute, if you were there with me, why didn't you tell me the meaning of the encounter with the serpent?" Annie said you could interpret such things, but that *she* couldn't." "That's almost right Chris, it's not that she *couldn't*, it's just that she *wouldn't*. That's how much she loved you. The fact that the serpent had more than one head meant that you had choices to make in your life. You stubbornly chose a misconceived duty and stuck with it. Twelve heads on the beast meant twelve months to make things right, or not. If not, then you will have orchestrated your own demise, twelve months to the day. Sorry, but that is the downside of free will. Annie knew this after you told her of your dream, she has the same gift as I once had. But Annie is not like me, it frightened her, only you could have saved yourself."

"How did Annie find out what happened to me?" "I'll show you Chris." Without moving toward the window, he waved his arm once again and the window curtain opened to reveal a blurry image of my house and a car pulling up. Becoming most clear now, "Oh my gosh it's Annie getting out of the GTO and walking up our brick path. There's my mother answering the door!" "My daughter had already told both of your parents about the feelings that you shared." "When was that?" "Before the second winter Chris. After your arrival at Firebase you stopped writing her, leaving her confused and then worried about your safety, so she called them to check on you."

"Look Hans, she brought me flowers." "Again Annie's asking about you and your mom is inviting her in, taking a seat on your couch. It looks like she is offering Annie something to eat or drink, but she shakes her head no. Knowing what might happen, you see your mom taking a seat on the couch next to Annie."

"But Annie's crying. What happened? "Yes, she's crying, what did you expect? Your mom has told her of your death. Annie now knows that you'll never return." "Hans, I can't bear to see her in pain. Now mom's crying too." "Chris, there is some good in this, they are finding comfort in each other. It's all about the ones that we leave behind. Annie may not understand it yet, but she will be with you again when she is called by the Father." "Look Hans, they're going upstairs to my room. I was there in my room, when she knelt at the bed, look she laid the flowers down, the lily-of-the valley, just like I remember." "No Chris, you weren't there, you were with me."

"On our side there is no 'yesterday and today,' but if it helps you understand, you are getting confused by my providing you with a vision of Annie coming to the hospital. I wanted to make sure that would agree to return to Shandalee and see your friends, so you could finally free yourself from the things that still bound you here on earth. Not to worry, the best part is yet to come, watch."

"She's leaving my house with my mom, where are they going?" "Just watch." "Oh my, that's Annie's mother getting out of the car, she looks like Annie, or Annie looks like her, you know." "Yes they do, but Annie is introducing them, didn't I tell you the best was yet to come?" "What, they're hugging each other, mom's not a hugger." "She is now

Chris. As a matter of fact, both of the sets of parents became the very best of friends over the past year, Annie too! They even went to Annie's high school graduation. Isn't that nice?" "It's wonderful Hans, thank you for showing me all this." I should have cried but there were no tears to be shed, instead I felt the greatest of joys to have been loved by Annie, deeply loved. "Goodbye my sweet Annie."

It was then that I felt an unfamiliar serenity baptize me in the name of the Father, replacing all of my fears, regrets and misaligned duty with a new and everlasting peace of mind. "Chris, are you ready? It's time to go." "Yes Hans, I'm ready." "Chris, Peter, in the name of the Father, Son and Holy Spirit I now release you to The Highest Place."

And in their final earthly act, the three of them, Hans, Chris, and Peter, with arms locked, were lifted to their heavenly home to join the righteous.

# The End

# "Hardscrabble Road"
## (Music and Lyrics by Max Yasgur Bonaventure)

"The times were high on Hardscrabble Road, most of us were there. Bobby and Janie and Gina and me, were chugging them down without care. It's been three long years, since we got together, and this was the place to be, the music was cranked, the drinks were big, and the girls got in for free.

*Come on down to Hardscrabble Road, for fun and friends to see,*
*it was a twist of fate one special night that brought my love to me.*

We're waiting for Sherry and her boyfriend Jerry, who always seems to be late. Funny thing is, I was there when they met, on a high school double blind date. Sherry I like, more than I should, who stayed with Jerry these years. He was rough and tough, a dealer we think, and likes his ice cold beers.

*Come on down to Hardscrabble Road, for fun and friends to see,*
*it was a twist of fate one special night that brought my love to me.*

They blew in lookin' scared to death, chased by a mangy dog of a man. Bobby and Janie and Gina and me, knew this wasn't part of our plan. Then, pow-pow-pow, and Jerry went down, as he took a bullet to his head. I grabbed for Sherry and pushed her aside, and thought she might be dead.

Now charging at me, was this crazed low-life, swinging his gun around. I knew my life, was next in line, instead of our night on-the-town. So I hit him hard, our bodies colliding, but it wasn't very long. The pain was sharp, and hurt a lot, and knew something was so wrong.

*Come on down to Hardscrabble Road, for fun and friends to see,*
*it was a twist of fate one special night that brought my love to me.*

I don't remember too much more, but figured it was all about cash. As his gun went flying, I lay dying, on this piece of human trash. Hardscrabble Road had taken its toll, in lives and love and greed. And the girl of my dreams, Sherry you know, now takes care of all my needs.

For in the pushing and shoving that night, a bullet changed my life, into my back, to walk no more, but Sherry's now my wife.

*Come on down to Hardscrabble Road, for fun and friends to see,*
*it was a twist of fate one special night that brought my love to me."*

# "Gingko Tree"
## (Music by Max Yasgur Bonaventure, Lyrics by Annie Ward)

*"Our time was short, as he professed to me,*
*his vow of love, under the gingko tree.*
*No tears of joy, could wash away,*
*duty's call, that September day.*

I'll remember the tree, and what it meant,
to love no other, but off he went.
A familiar breeze, blew its leaves today,
that whispered his name, while still away.

*Our time was short, as he professed to me,*
*his vow of love, under the gingko tree.*
*No tears of joy, could wash away,*
*duty's call, that September day.*

The world knew well of the struggle he faced,
but we prayed for him in that jungle place.

News came quick, and was a mortal blow,
to our new love, soldiers told us so.
I kept his wish, and another vow did make,
I'll meet you at the gingko on another day!

*Our time was short, as he professed to me,*
*his vow of love, under the gingko tree.*
*No tears of joy, could wash away,*
*duty's call, that September day.*

Under the gingko tree.
Our vow of love under the gingko tree."

# Additional novels by JF Krizan

# My Juxtaposition: Not Just another Willy Loman

**What happens when much that you believe in and hope for is counter to the prevailing attitude and actions of others? The larger the divide the greater the juxtaposition for all those involved.**

# ALL THAT WE EVER KNEW: THE RECONCILIATION OF GOD AND SCIENCE

"Thus, if God created everything, did he not create science? Certainly science did not create God. Similarly, Hawking's statement that, 'God is not necessary (in creation),' also means that he *may* have been the initiator. So what is it, God or science or could we be talking about the same thing? Peter, whether by intent or not, you have created a paradox for all sides."

**Excerpt from "All That We Ever Knew."**

Made in the USA
Middletown, DE
03 July 2020